Blue Pencils
Volume II

Edited by:

Charlie Wilson and Leslie Sextius

ISBN: 978-1-9164916-0-1

DEDICATION

This book is dedicated to our backers, without whom we wouldn't be able to share these wonderful, creative, heart-breaking and wacky stories with you. So thank you to: Paul Sturges, DeAnn Bell, Maeve Kenny, Tanniea Powell, Marion and Ken Balmforth, Vicky Williams, Sue Jennings, Becky Taylor, Eimear Lawlor, Philippa Grand, Eoin Murray, Raymonde Arcens-Wilson, Dawn Wood, Rose Cantrell, Hazel Johnson, Sarah Johnson, Katie Wood, Lyle Skains, Jean Roberts and Gill Parys.

CONTENTS

FROM THE EDITORS

This book has been a labour of love for us. We have both had hundreds of other things to do, and about 90% of them would have been more appropriate uses of our time, but the thing about writing is that it's a bug you can't quite give up. And after editing and publishing Volume I, we weren't quite ready to stop.

The stories here are chosen from submissions sent to us from across the country (and the world). They are stories that spoke to us with strong, unique voices, and said something that resonated with us. We hope they resonate with you, too.

Charlie Wilson and Leslie Sextius, 2018

FREE BIRD
Rose Cantrell

The last time I saw her was on the station at Chiuso just before dawn in the sharp chill of January. Heavy snow had continued to fall throughout the night but it did not deter the alpine train. The murky glow of headlights peered through the darkness right on time, the snowflakes large and bright in their beam.

She gave me a quick hug as she turned towards the train. I watched her slender back, envying her casual grace, remembering her knock-kneed youth with a faint smile. Where did all those years go? How did my little duckling become a swan with a past? Flakes of snow haloed her dark hair as she disappeared into the train. My own words from yesterday grated through my mind. 'Take care! Don't leave someone else to pick up the pieces.'

It sounded selfish and heartless to me now. This free bird, to whom 'taking care' was just another limit to her freedom.

I stood alone on the cold station platform. My mind's eye sought new realisations through the fall of snowflakes in the dim light. I must have unconsciously expected my daughter to be like me, share my interests, my views. For some reason I hung onto those expectations. She didn't even recognise them. Her attitudes were a strange land to me, alien and hostile. I had no map, no compass.

I had always loved her in spite of arguments and absences, but sometimes even being loved seemed to weigh her down. Broken chains of relationships trailed her. She would stay as long as things were going where she wanted, but that required constant change in itself as what she wanted changed. She travelled all over the world finding different loves, drove to India, trekked New Zealand, camper-vanned the States, bummed Thailand, Vietnam, Philippines and more.

When it came to settling down, she would play the game for a while. Try to be a 'normal' person, fit in with a job and domestic routines – to a degree. But gradually, the captivity would weigh her down. The links would strain and finally snap and she would hurtle into an emotional barrage of self-doubt. Confused, lost and alone, she would perhaps come back to me to heal.

It would take me less than a few seconds of the initial phone call to recognise the heart-sinking angst in her voice, the slight choke as she soul-searched and raged. Still encased in my own issues and plans, I listened. Did I? Listen? With moist eyes and tight lips, what I actually heard was distorted by sadness, frustration, my own guilt.

When she came home, the joy at seeing each other was genuine. The concern for her troubles was sincere. We would walk and talk, eat and laugh. For a while we would bask in that mutual warmth. We would be close and then a window would open and a fresh breeze would ruffle her wing feathers and off she would go again, whisked away on a whirlwind high.

In new surroundings, keen to get it right this time, her initial communications with me could be ecstatic and exhilarated, carried away with the sheer joy of living, and I would rejoice in her happiness and pray it would last.

All too often the fresh breeze became a tornado that, having swept her away, would drop her and leave her in a crumpled heap that my heart ached on finding. I would try to help with practical talk about home, security, steady income, and then wish I hadn't because of the frustration it caused us both.

I would start gently with "Why don't you..."

"Mum, that's not what I want."

As time passed, I would progress to "If you would just..."

"Mum why can't you see I don't need that hassle?"

Then later, fretting and tense "If you would only..."

The backlash trigger was extremely sensitive. We both knew it.

"What part of no don't you understand? I don't fit in your rut. You could fly if you didn't cling so desperately to the ground. Life's for exploring not being chained down with debt and aggravation. Don't do that to me!"

Then steel would flash. We'd circle each other, armour on, weapons drawn in defence more than attack, neither of us understanding why the other didn't understand. Our wounds were common but unshared.

She was different in a way I couldn't reach, couldn't echo, mimic or follow. I could only observe with tight lips and fearful resignation.

I blinked away the snow on my eyelashes, watching her now through the train window as she walked through the carriage and found a seat. My free bird, caged in a railway carriage, on the move to new and different pastures.

Greener grass? I hoped so.

Already I could hear her voice, full of the wonder and enthusiasm with which she would greet the new experience. Who could resist the joy of hearing the happiness in her voice! The relief of knowing she was enjoying life. The rising of hope, the lifting of responsibility, the floating away of weight and worry. And my daughter at her loveliest, full of talk about new people, new perspectives, new dreams of the future, yearning to share the joy. My mixture of fascination and fear as I listened to her accounts of adventures, trips to high-risk places, problems solved by wit and will, the constant change and challenge that fed her energy. And me in that alien mental landscape, trying to enthuse and encourage and all the while suppressing an urgent need to pull her back from the edge, like a toddler on a cliff top. A kiss, a tickle, a cuddle and all would be well, wouldn't it?

Over and over my familiar prayers for her safety and happiness clashed with memories of the surprised anger in her voice when things started to go wrong. The protesting agony as another castle of hope caved in on itself. It was not failure. What pushed her over the edge was disappointment, frustration, anger, sometimes heartache. She would return feeling weary and vulnerable. It allowed me in. I had a part to play in her life again, temporarily.

In reality she was strong. She took the blows and bounced back and I stepped away and hoped, always guilty that I hadn't done enough, never enough. Yet I never got 'doing more' right. It led to stinging resentment that was harder to live with than guilt.

She knew I was standing on the dimly lit platform, the snow falling around me silent and unheeded. She did not look until the whistle blew and the train jerked forward. Then she blew me a kiss. I waved and watched through floating white as the train pulled away and another little piece of my heart de-materialised into the snowy twilight.

FISH IS GOOD FOR YOU
Karen Adcock

Pole, Scrubb and Puddleglum the Marsh-wiggle had paused at the summit, the valley-land of Narnia lingering warm and comforting at their backs, but resolutely they set their faces to the North and the vast, lonely unknown of Ettinsmoor...

"Flippin' 'eck! Car'n I have nothing for myself?"

Mum's voice was loud enough to break into the wild waste lands and drag Lisa back from the ancient giants of Harfang to Thursday teatime — usually the tempting aroma of sausage, mash and fried onions was a more subtle shuffle across a literary divide.

Billy's face crumpled as Mum's harsh tone cut across his whinging and she held up an authoritative finger.

"Doh even think about blartin."

There was much blinking and sniffing, but at least no further bawling from the four-year-old.

Lisa's attention was drawn to an odd looking package on the big, wooden table next to her. She had never seen anything this particular shade of rusty orange and wondered about the significance of the bright yellow, daisy shaped object she could see sitting in the middle of it. It was very tempting just to sneak a little touch, but yuk! It was a squidgy, plastic wrapped — something. The question forming on her lips remained unasked as Dad came through the door from work and the teatime cacophony began.

Dad picked up the package. "Kippers, love? Unusual."

"Just fancied something different, that's all. Got any fags?"

Dad ferreted in his pockets, eventually bringing out a pack of Park Drive. Drawing the cigarettes out of the sophisticated red and white box, he tapped them both on the packet, then up-ended them and tapped the other end. It seemed an odd thing to do, but he always did it. Lighting the two

4

together he passed one over, and in a choreographed ritual they both inhaled deeply and exhaled slowly; a reward for their respective hard work and a signal for the children that this was the beginning of grown-up time.

"Don't blame me for the consequences," he said, handing Mum the package, then turned aside to pick up the youngest of the bunch, happily playing with saucepan lids in the enamel bath on the hearth.

Mum shrugged and disappeared into the kitchen to drop the mysterious package into a pan of boiling water. Lisa had so many questions but, wisely for a seven-year-old, decided to keep quiet and just watch.

Deftly Mum spread two pieces of bread with VG margarine, cut them in half (posh triangles) and arranged them on a plate. The package, retrieved and opened with great care, unleashed its pungency with no warning, the aroma seeming to trickle off the table and attach itself to any available surface.

Billy stopped clamouring for a taste and turned back for his bottle of tea; he wasn't ready for such foul smelling adventures.

Mum pushed the plate towards Lisa. Cautiously she took some onto the fork, causing Mum to laughingly goad her, "Goo on, get it down yer neck, it wo ert yer! Fish is s'posed to be good for yer."

Swallowing quickly to avoid as much of the taste as possible, Lisa choked, and began to cough and wretch, tears coursing down her cheeks.

"Arthur! Give us 'an 'and love. I think she's got a fish bone stuck!"

"Give 'er a drink o' water… or try some dry bread," was Dad's best advice.

Mum ran next door to Mr Long's — "A man who knew a lot about a lot," according to everyone on the street.

"Make her cough," he said with certainty. But nothing would shift it.

"Perhaps she's swallowed it, and it scratched her throat on the way down?" However, inspection with a torch, (following the usual hunt for SP2 batteries) revealed there was indeed a foreign body.

Lisa began to cry at the thought of a body in her throat, but only a little because sobbing made it move up and down, which really hurt. Meanwhile the adults fussed around discussing the practicalities of bus timetables and shortcuts to the hospital.

***

And so it was that seven o'clock on a dark Thursday evening saw them heading into the centre of Wolverhampton on a bumpy, smelly bus, with cold leather seats. Mum made them sit upstairs so she could have a fag on the way to calm her nerves. Lisa shrank into the corner of the seat, trying to escape the eye-watering smoke that seemed attracted to her and trying not to antagonise her mum further – she was already cross at having been made to miss The Archers.

"Yow'm up late me wench," said an old man as they got off the bus, but Mum ignored him. It was bad enough having to do this, without nosy old men making comments. Clutching her chiffon headscarf tightly under her chin, she grabbed her daughter's hand and set off at a purposeful speed, forcing the youngster into a trot to keep up.

The wind kept pace with them as they hurried across the back end of town and, as the outline of St George's tall steeple filled their vision, they paused to catch their breath.

Huddled against the boundary wall for shelter, Mum lit another fag; the friendly orange glow from the tip illuminated Mum's face, and Lisa noticed that she looked a bit scared too. She thought about Pole and Scrubb and wondered if Aslan was real – and really hoped he was. The thoughts distracted her a little as they entered the unlit churchyard and she didn't notice the soft scuffling noises from the abattoir on the other side of the low wall until a disembodied, low-pitched wail set them fleeing towards the safety of the main road and the welcome sight of the hospital in the distance.

**

A stern looking lady in the casualty reception was asking Mum lots of questions, whilst everyone around listened to the answers; some were pretending not to take any notice but others were almost active participants.

"That's down the Low-'ill estate, aye it?' as she gave the address.

"Yeah – you wouldn't wanna be wanderin' round there at this time o' night."

"Must be serious," commented someone else.

Then all went quiet as seasoned attenders waited for the all-important "What seems to be the problem?"

Mum suddenly let go of her tight grip on Lisa's hand and fished in her coat pocket for a handkerchief. Lisa looked up, about to ask a question but remained silent as she saw a tear roll down Mum's cheek. She wasn't old enough to read this sort of story: the one that told of a no-hope-life with three youngsters and a fourth on the way, no money, the constant battle of robbing Peter to pay Paul and now the fear of being judged for giving her child kippers when she should have been eating bangers and mash and sticky fried onions. It was an adult tale — no mention of magic or kind fairies, only wastelands and giants.

**

"Lisa! Lisa! C'mon, it's time to get up. Yer gonna be late for school." Mum was shouting from the bottom of the stairs, vainly trying to streamline the morning routine and failing miserably. Yet again the kids would have to make do with a bottle of tea as they rushed up the road with no breakfast.

A sharp pain as she swallowed and a screwed up tissue cocooning the offending foreign body reminded Lisa of the drama last night. She didn't want to get out of her warm bed, but Mum's voice was very insistent. The veiled threat of the 'school-board man' was the final persuader and she quickly grabbed the tissue to show her teacher, Miss Knight.

Mum was waiting in the kitchen, bottle of the dreaded pink medicine in one hand and surely the largest teaspoon ever in the other. Even squeezing your nose really hard didn't stop the reflex shudder as it trickled down your gullet.

Her teacher was obligingly sympathetic as she listened to the tale of the scary noises in the churchyard and the long walk through green tiled corridors that smelled like sick and Dettol mixed together. She was curious about the fish tanks in the Casualty department, wanting to know how many fish and what colour? She laughed when Lisa told her about the doctor in his white coat who had told her a joke and was suitably nervous at the mention of long handled crocodile forceps. Best of all was her reaction to the unveiling of 'the foreign body' – a sharp intake of breath as she gave Lisa a hug saying, "Ooh my brave girl; your mom must have been very proud."

Standing in the dinner queue later, surrounded by laughing and squealing little girls as she repeated her tale, Lisa suddenly remembered that today was Friday – and it was always fish-fingers for dinner.

A CUP OF TEA
Synne Johnsson

She put two spoons of sugar in her tea and stirred it. The clanking filled the silent room with sound like a distant church bell. The spoon looked big between her wrinkled fingers. She always put the milk in before the water, which used to make me cringe. Now I was just happy to see that she had kept a few characteristics from her old self.

The room had started off completely white. White walls, white bed, white table. The only thing standing out was a long, red string hanging by the bed, for my mum to pull in if she needed help. We'd added some colour recently: on the table there was a light pink embroidery cloth and a tiny yellow vase with some flowers my nephew picked for her from my brother's garden. When she moved in she had insisted on having the white cloth one, but we eventually agreed that it would be nicer with some colour. Her bed was covered with a light blue, flowery bedspread and two purple velvet pillows we had brought from her house. Above it was a replica of Edvard Munch's Madonna. My mum had bought it ages ago from a charity shop in Camden. My dad hated it, but everyone knew that that didn't matter. The painting was going up on the wall and there was no point in arguing about it. All over her room there were drawings my nephews had made for her. An orange cat, a house, a horse. Typical children's drawings. On her bedside table was a family photo we took at a photographer two years ago.

"How are you? Everything alright here?" I asked and she looked at me with empty, confused eyes. They were as dark as mine. I'd always been proud of having my mother's eyes.

"Everything is great! It's such a lovely hotel," she said with her rusty voice. "Yesterday we went to a lovely restaurant, Jacob and I. We had this wonderful wine from France and I had a lovely steak and a so-called 'tiramisu'."

I sighed. She'd become so old over the last few years. There wasn't a single piece of hair that had stayed young. It was all just as white as the walls in her room.

"Uhm..." Last time I visited, I told her that she was talking nonsense and that she was actually in an elderly home, and I was her daughter. She'd become extremely angry and shouted at both the nurses and me. So now I ignored it.

"Well... I'm glad to hear that you're okay," I said.

"Yes," she said and took a sip of her tea. "Very good indeed."

How I missed having a mum. I missed having someone to call when I didn't know what washing programme I should wash my clothes on, or when I had been fighting with my boyfriend. I missed having someone who took care of me.

I felt a bit guilty. She had never been too busy to look after my brother and me, but now, when she needed help and caring, we had sent her here. I knew she would have refused to let us take care of her and how much she hated to be a burden, but a part of me still felt like we had let her down. She had done everything for us before she got sick. Drove us wherever we wanted, made us dinner, bought us everything we needed. Never had she demanded anything from us in return, except for the few minutes it took to do the dishes. The only request she had ever made was that when she got old, could we please find an elderly home where she was allowed to have a glass of wine or two on a Friday evening.

Her room kind of reminded me of my room in halls where I lived my first year of university. She drove me there to help me get settled. She helped me make my small room more homely and nice and bought me everything I needed and a few things I didn't need. I remember that she cried when she was leaving and I almost got annoyed at her because it made me feel guilty.

"Okay then..." she said, when we had unpacked everything.

"Okay then," I said.

"I guess you're all settled now, huh?" my mum said, looking around my awfully small room. She didn't say it then, but later she told me how heart breaking she thought it was leaving me in a room as small and plain.

"Yeah, it looks nice, don't you think?"

"It does," she smiled. I could hear the lump in her throat and her eyes were tearing up. "I better get back so I don't get home too late. Work tomorrow."

"I know. That's okay. Thank you for all the help though."

"That's the least a mum can do, isn't it?"

We walked out to the car together and when we were there my mum hugged me. She had stopped trying to hold her tears back and her whole face was red. We said goodbye and my mum drove home to a house where her daughter didn't live anymore. Now I was the one who cried when I left.

***

"So have Thomas and his boys visited you lately? Luke is five next month and he is extremely excited." She didn't reply. "He's going to have a birthday party, but I guess they've already invited you?"

I let my mouth run away with me even though I knew very well she didn't recognise us anymore. And that *of course* she didn't remember being invited to a birthday party. Last time she remembered me was a little over a year ago. She told me that I looked nice with short hair and that I had to stop biting my nails. How annoying I used to think it was when she commented on my nails. But not anymore.

"Luke looks exactly like Thomas, right?" Nothing. She just stared out in the air. It looked like she was staring at the painting behind me. She lifted her cup to take a sip of her tea but it slipped in her shaky hands and she spilled tea all over herself.

"Here, Mum, let me help," I started, reaching out to dab at her blouse.

"No," she said. "No! Get away – get away – get away from me!" I dropped the napkins back onto the table and stepped back. She was tearing up, hands flapping feebly in the air in front of her, and I sighed, sinking back into my seat.

The first time she got angry with me like that we were at our local supermarket, buying food for Christmas. Everything had gone smoothly, but when we were going to pay she just stood there, looking at the notes in her purse. She picked up a tenner and gave it to the woman behind the cashier.

"I need another twenty pounds, miss," the woman had said, but my mum had just stared on her purse.

"Mum, just give her the twenty note right there," I had said and reached for her purse. She had quickly moved it away from me.

"I don't need your help, Caroline!" she snapped. "Do you think I'm stupid? I'm perfectly fine without you!" I was shocked, not able to understand why she'd been so angry. "You're such a know-it-all!" The words had hurt me. She'd never spoken to me that rudely before. I had gone to the car, angry and confused, leaving her to deal with the money herself.

She hadn't wanted help then and she didn't want it now, even though it looked like she needed it. She struggled with wiping tea off her flowery blouse, and eventually gave up. She was dressed nicely, which had made me smile when I walked into her room. She'd always been a little vain, so I knew she would have appreciated that the nurses was careful with the choice of clothes to dress her in. She was even wearing a little make-up.

"I got an interview for a new job on Thursday," I said, trying to get her to focus on something else. "And David, my boyfriend, just got a raise! Isn't that great? He wanted to come with me today, but unfortunately he had a football match." She didn't answer, just stared out the window. I wondered what she was thinking. Where she was. What she saw outside. I was wondering if, in her head, she really had experienced all the things she thought or if it started as an already false memory.

"Should I make you another cup of tea?" I asked and bit a piece of nail from my ring finger.

She glanced towards me and fondness flashed across her face for a few seconds. "You really have to stop biting your nails, Caroline."

It came like rain from a blue sky. She remembered me. She actually remembered me. I started to cry, eyes welling up, and I didn't even try to hold it back. Never had I been happier to hear her say those words. I looked at her and saw my mum. The mum who had dropped me off at university years before. The mum who had ignored my dad when he asked why on earth we were going to have a painting of a naked woman on the wall in our sitting room. The mum whose only wish was to be able to drink a glass of wine in the elderly home. With tears dripping down my chin I took her wrinkled hand and squeezed it. "I will, Mum. I will."

AN AFTERNOON AT ST. PANCRAS
Sarah Johnson

It's a weekday afternoon at St Pancras Station and the platform is bustling with people. I fold into the crowds coming off the train, careful to keep out of the way of anyone in a hurry and make my way towards the concourse. Ahead of me, a girl struggles to keep control of her wayward suitcase, which is missing a wheel. After it flips over for the third time, she gives up trying to drag it and picks it up by the handle, heading purposefully in the direction of the main station. I follow her towards the gates and, as we get closer, the hum of trains lurching in and out of the platforms fades and the chatter of commuters enjoying their lunch grows louder.

Even at this time, the station is busy: full of tourists with their heads stuck in tube maps and people rushing through on their phones, their minds preoccupied with where they're going. Despite this, the atmosphere around the shops is lazy. Next to me, a group of friends hug excitedly as they get ready to go on a long awaited girls' weekend and businessmen sit around in stiff black suits reading broadsheet newspapers and sipping espressos. I have some time on my hands and grab a drink in the nearest cafe. Settling down at one of the tables outside with a latte and a chocolate muffin, I watch the comings and goings.

I'm sat opposite the exit gates of St Pancras International. There are a growing number of cab drivers gathering in front of me, their white signs drooping with boredom as they wait for the delayed 14:22. As the holidaymakers finally begin trickling through the doors, the unmistakable sound of a piano begins drifting over the crowds, turning heads up and down the concourse. I follow their gazes and find it hidden underneath the stairs opposite me. An old man sits at it, testing out the keys. His thin white hair is almost translucent in the pale light and stands up on top of his head in wisps. His face, lined with age, is pensive as he chooses what to play. Before he begins, he takes a moment to carefully turn up the cuffs of his cardigan. One or two strings have unravelled from inside the sleeve and hang down by his wrists like red spaghetti.

The melody he chooses is slow and expressive and the chords float through the air like leaves in the wind. He closes his eyes and lets the music take him somewhere else. Despite his joints being swollen with arthritis, his fingers move across the keys effortlessly, guided by the vibrating strings inside the piano. When he hits a particularly poignant chord, he frowns, the lines around his eyes deepening and holds there for a second before the music gently sweeps him away again.

By now, he has caught the attention of several passers-by who stop briefly on their way through the station to watch him. One boy is so enamoured, it takes his mum several attempts to get him to move on, her eyes glancing nervously at the departures board every few seconds. Others just stop to film him, their eyes glued to their screens rather than the man himself. Meanwhile the music is consuming me, making the hairs on my arms stand on end and my fingertips itch.

Seamlessly, the music shifts into a new tempo and the tone changes; it's happier and more nostalgic but holds a sense of loss. The man takes on a new lease of life as his body twists with the music, thrumming with energy as the melody dances towards its climax, his whole body holding a new air of confidence.

"He plays beautifully doesn't he?"

I jump and look up to see a woman standing beside me, her eyes fixed on the man at the piano. She's around seventy-five, slightly plump and wears her hair in a tight grey perm.

"Never fails to take my breath away." She sighs and looks away, gesturing to the seat opposite me. "May I?"

I nod. She moves the chair around so that she can still see the piano and lowers herself onto it carefully. We sit in silence beside each other, listening contentedly.

"Does he come here often?" I ask quietly.

"Every day, without fail."

"He's mesmerising to watch."

She nods. "Always has been. I couldn't take my eyes off him the first time." She shifts beside me, settling into her seat. "I was eighteen and on my way home from work. There I was, walking through the station minding my own business when this lively piano tune started up out of nowhere."

She smiles at me, a twinkle in her eye. "He was always playing something cheeky back then, flashing his big grin at everyone who passed and winking at the girls. I liked to watch him from the shadows, always taking a moment to listen on my way past. Then one day, I was watching from my usual spot when he looked right at me. It was like being hit by a bolt of lightning."

Her voice breaks and she goes quiet, fiddling with her thumbs on top of her handbag.

"That's beautiful," I say.

She's smiling but there's a wet sheen to her eyes. "He doesn't even recognise me now."

I have to swallow around a sudden lump in my throat. "I'm so sorry," I say.

"These things happen to the best of us," she says. "I'm only glad that I can still come here and see him play, like it was back then." She lets out a small sigh, her breath a little steadier.

I look back over at the man, trying to imagine who he used to be and the lump in my throat grows a little. I'm suddenly aware that the tannoy is calling the three o'clock train and I glance at the digital clock above the departures board.

"Oh my god, is that the time? I'm going to be so late," I say, rushing to pack up my things.

The lady laughs and stoops to pick up the ticket I've dropped.

"Thank you," I say with a smile. "It was lovely to meet you."

"And you," she says.

We exchange a final look of farewell and I join the throng of people hurrying towards the tube. I strain my ears to listen to the man's playing until it is finally swallowed by the noise of the station.

***

A few hours later, I'm stood backstage waiting to go on, nerves coursing through my body. My mind wanders back to the pianist and how confident he looked sat in the middle of the station, oblivious to his surroundings. Out in the auditorium, the crowd's excited whispers begin to die down and I can hear a soft applause begin to ripple through the audience. I take a deep breath and flex my fingers, hoping that some of the man's confidence has rubbed off on me. I step out into the light and my heart rate quickens. The applause dies down as I walk across the stage and take my seat at the piano. For a moment, I let my fingers hover over the keys. Then I begin to play.

THE ARRANGEMENT
Fiona Dye

"Can you be discreet?"

The text arrived less than forty minutes after they'd parted ways. On reading it, excitement fizzed through her veins — mixing with the Prosecco and Espresso Martinis she'd had over lunch. Their fourth meeting. She liked him more each time.

She could be discreet. Lucky for him.

Of course, the question didn't mean only what was written. It was an invitation.

She knew she should turn him down; that would be the right thing to do.

"Yes, I can," she messaged back.

His reply was almost instant. "I'm in the West Mids, week after next. Are you free any time then?"

She was disappointed that the message was purely about the practicalities. She had wanted him to flirt a little more, like he had when they'd met. That would have felt right.

Still, she checked her diary, and replied, "Wednesday that week possible. Meet for lunch again, or, I could work from home?"

"Yes. Do that. I'll get to yours about 12.30."

And so, it was arranged. In five short texts.

There was the occasional flurry of messages between them in the following days, and the morning he was due she felt sick with nerves.

"See you later," was all he'd texted earlier. He could have been confirming a business appointment. Despite that, she felt her skin flush, the heat pricking at her neck and cheeks. She closed her eyes, breathed deeply, trying to slow down her heartbeat and quell the sickness. Ashamed and thrilled. It was too late to back out now, and anyway, she didn't really want to.

"Me, too," she messaged back, adding a smiley blowing a kiss.

Five minutes later and she had convinced herself she'd got things wrong, that once he arrived he'd say she'd misunderstood, he really was just here to talk through her investment plans. She read the few other texts she had received from him; logic told her they could mean only one thing, but still, she read them over and over again. To be sure.

Her preparations were painstaking. She washed her hair, took a leisurely bath, laid out the clothes she was planning to wear. Considered just a robe. Changed her selection twice. She interspersed these activities with brief moments of action at her laptop, sending the occasional email to colleagues and business partners in order to convince herself she really was working from home. It didn't help with the guilt, though she was unsure what she felt most guilty about, the planned rendezvous or lying to her boss and friends at work.

By 12.15 she was ready. Underneath her dress she had on the full set of matching underwear she had bought from Agent Provocateur the previous year. It had cost almost an entire month's mortgage payment. When she bought it, she had envisaged a life of new and exciting relationships. Romantic. Enticing. As it was, she'd only had chance to wear it once in the past twelve months. Cost per wear, it was currently proving to be something of a bad buy.

Ten minutes after he was due to arrive, she received another message. "Sorry, motorway a nightmare. With you in 15."

"Ok," she pinged back.

She thought about putting the kettle on. She'd not had breakfast, that early nausea had ruled that out, and by now she was getting hungry, but the thought of sex on a full stomach didn't appeal. A cup of tea would have to do, take the edge off her appetite. But the kettle had no sooner boiled than there was a knock on the door. For one moment, she thought she wouldn't answer it: it couldn't be him and, if it was, then here was the last chance to change her mind. To be better. Even whilst she was thinking that, she was walking towards the door, reaching for the door knob.

"Hi," he said. "Didn't take me quite as long as I thought to do that last bit."

"Hi. Good to see you. Come on in."

And that was the full extent of the small talk.

Then it was the kissing and the touching, and the pulling together, and then the parting so he could remove his coat and shoes, and the coming back together, and more kissing and holding. Exploring. Pulling in tight, hips and thighs merging. Wet lips, urgent tongues, and hot, quick breath freshened by recently chewed gum. They smiled when they finally broke apart, and for a moment just looked.

She led him to the stairs, picking up the bottle of Merlot and two glasses from the dining room table as she went past. Once upstairs, he asked a little bashfully if he could use the toilet. She was relieved to hear him wash his hands afterwards. By the time he came out of the bathroom she was lying on the bed, the duvet just covering her feet, the underwear and stockings reconfirming her intentions. An agent provocateur indeed.

The sex was great. Afterwards, he held her. She let him.

Later, as he was getting ready to leave, he became serious.

"You know, this is just a bit of fun, right? I think you're great and everything, but I love my girlfriend and our kids. I'm not looking to replace them. If she and I were to split, I wouldn't be looking to start another relationship. You do get that, right?"

He spoke confidently enough, though he didn't look at her once whilst he was talking.

She didn't look at him either. She wanted to laugh. Really laugh. She thought about the sex, so she didn't.

THESE DAYS
Charlie Wilson

**You: I miss you so much but sometimes I s2g I
just want to punch you in your stupid smile**

She hesitates, finger hovering over the 'send' button. Behind her, the bar spills out onto the street, throbbing music echoing across her shoulders and up into the base of her skull, a pounding pressure that she shuts her eyes against.

Her friends are waiting for her. She begged off for a moment, citing the tacky sweat she was drenched in as an excuse for wanting air. Now she's outside, the lack of movement is making her feel sick. Inside it's so easy to let it wash over her, heat and bodies and alcohol in one blur of sensation. Out here the cold air leans on her like fingers pressing on her shoulders and forearms, gripping her tightly.

She can't send it. But it's nice to write it down.

You:

The blank message taunts her. There are so many things she could say. So many things that start with *I love you* and *I miss you*, but even more that start with *how could you?* and *I hate you* and *every time I think about you I think I'm going to die because I can't breathe —*

It's a work in progress. She stares down at the phone and thinks about all the things she wants to send.

"Li? You coming?"

She doesn't look up. Instead, she locks the screen and slides it into her bra because this outfit has no pockets. Then, and only then, does she look over her shoulder and smile at Ana, who's standing in the doorway and framed with light, a shadow cast against the neon of the bar, dark hair and dark skin and dark clothes in contrast to the blues and pinks of the evening behind her.

"Li?" she asks again. Li dredges a smile from the corner of her mind, a

18

little dusty and broken but still good, and offers it to her friend.

"Coming," Li says and heads back inside. The pressure doesn't let up when the air turns from frigid to humid, but it's easier to ignore with Ana at her side.

***

The before goes something like this:

"–the most selfish person on the planet–"

"Don't think I don't know the truth, Li–"

"The truth?" She says it on a laugh, breathless and angry and disbelieving, and he stops and stares at her, waiting. "You think the truth matters here? Since when has the truth ever mattered to us, Ben?"

"I didn't touch her," he tells her, brown eyes soulful and injured, just watery enough for Li to know that he means this, that he's fighting back tears at her words. "You know I wouldn't. You, on the other hand–"

"You don't get to tell me what I did," she snarls, hands fisted into her hair and pulling, revelling in the sharp, insistent throbbing it leaves behind. "I know what I did! Three years ago–"

"And I forgave you–"

"And you never let me forget it–"

He pushes away from her, storming to their window and staring down from their building. His shoulders are hunched forward, the weight of the world and an angry girlfriend shoving them down into a semi-permanent slump. "I didn't touch her."

"But you want to," Li says. It's the truth. It doesn't matter though.

"And you still think of Isabella when we're in bed," he says. The words are harsh, but he just sounds defeated. She goes to him, crossing the floor between them on dancer's feet, and curls her arms around his waist, burying her face into his shoulder blades. His shirt is sweaty, because it's 30°C outside and he sweats when he's angry. It's damp against her face, but she loves him too much to pull away, even with the salt-musk heavy in her nostrils. He sighs, shuddering as he sags against her, and his hands come up to cover hers, squeezing them as she holds them against his stomach.

"We should get married."

"No, we shouldn't."

(When they look back at these days, later on, neither remembers who asks and who refuses. They both know that it was the right decision. But Li wishes she'd had the chance to take his name. She wishes – god, the things she wishes.)

***

In bed, Ana is a different creature. Daylight makes her sweet and demure, sarcastic but only in the casual, surface way that never gets sharper than wry and funny, never as bitter as the way words fall out of Li's mouth like fangs, snapping down on the closest piece of flesh, rending and tearing until she can taste blood. After the sun sets, Li lies back against her pillows and lets Ana take her apart with a calculated mix of expertise and enthusiasm, eyes sharp as Li shudders and sighs and moans. When Li returns the favour, Ana never looks quite as happy as she does when she's looming above Li, watching her, measuring her, examining her. It doesn't stop Li from returning the favour. That's not the sort of girl she is.

When people find out they're – what are they? Dating? Fucking? More, less? Li doesn't care enough to ask, these days. But when they find out, there are careful exchanges of looks between their friends, little 'can you believe that?' head tilts, and 'woah' eyebrows, and 'that's a bad idea' frowns. Li has to sit through three shovel talks, all but one from people she considers personal friends, and Ana sits through exactly none. It should hurt more than it does, but Li doesn't mind. When she tells Ana later, she gets laughter and sharp teeth grazing her belly.

"Are you going to break my heart, Wang Li?"

Li rolls her eyes and stretches out against the pillows, loving the brush of cotton against her bare skin. "You'd have to have a heart for me to do that, Anabella," she replies. Ana laughs again, low and husky, like the whiskey Ben would drink at his father's house, the two of them sitting in the back garden on a bench, looking out on a land-locked boat that neither of them knew how to sail but were sure they would take to sea one day.

"I have a heart, Li-Li," she promises, pupils so wide it's hard to distinguish between them and her irises. "Do you?"

No, Li thinks. *My heart shrivelled up years ago, curling up in an ashtray with our cigarette butts and I've never quite gotten rid of the smell.*

She smiles. "Why don't you try and find out?" She pulls Ana up and down, into her arms, and kisses her hard enough to taste blood.

***

Meeting Isabella was the start of the end, she knows, but she can't find it within herself to regret it. Isabella is everything that Li isn't: sweet, funny, genuine, beautiful – tall, blonde and the perfect princess as well, of course. But these days she has an undercut and three more piercings in her ears, and while she still takes time out of her day to talk to strangers on the street who look 'too sad to walk past', there's more purpose in her stride when they walk towards a café for lunch.

"You got places to be?" Li asks, eying the three-inch heels that make Isabella hit six foot.

"Always," Isabella tells her, tucking her phone into her bag and smiling at the children they walk past, one of whom stares at her as she marches onwards, caught in her orbit. Li sympathises. It's easy to do that. "Why, are you looking for somewhere to be?"

Always, Li thinks, but just shrugs and keeps quiet.

They drink coffee and chatter about their lives, and their friends' lives, and – more than anything – their random acquaintances' lives, because those are far more fun and far less emotionally compromising. So-and-so broke up with such-and-such, and the-guy-with-the-bald-patch asked out too-good-for-him and they *went out*, but only on one date because she was pitying him, and then three-sheets-to-the-wind went to AA and wishes-she-was-Kate-Middleton dropped out of her night classes because her schedule was 'just too busy'. It's simple gossip and Li hates that she loves it, but can't really work up enough energy to change the subject. She'll pay for it later, when she spends three hours tossing and turning in bed, wishing she was a better sort of person, the type who would have defended bald-patch and called up Kate Middleton to check on her.

But Li isn't that person, and Isabella has learnt to leave other people's business alone.

"Are you okay?" Isabella asks her as they walk out of the café, jackets firmly in place over their arms as they soak up the last of the summer rays. The September sun is starting to stutter and fail, and Li wishes she could hold onto it just for a few more days. She closes her eyes and looks up and lets the yellow fill her sight, warmth pressing against closed eyelids until Isabella takes her arm and steers her patiently out of the way of a family of five.

Li opens her eyes and lies. "I'm good, Isabella." She smiles. It comes easily enough, these days, but the cobwebs are still there under a thin veneer of chapstick and confidence. "Better than I've been in ages."

Isabella's face melts and she glows when she smiles at Li. "I'm so glad," she says. "I'm so glad."

***

The last box has been gaffa-taped and loaded away, into the back of a cupboard that Li doesn't plan on looking in until she moves. It's a shoebox apartment, but it's hers, and she doesn't exactly want a lot of furniture. There's space, and big windows that let the weak winter sun in, dancing across polished wood floors. On the wall, she can trace the cracks in the paint. Her iPod is set in its cradle, playing something slow and indie, a strong downbeat that pulls her towards it with both drumsticks. She turns it up and smiles, because she doesn't have neighbours here, not yet, and when she does she can tell them to go fuck themselves, the way she's always wanted to.

There are texts on her phone, but none more recently than four days ago. She doesn't check them. She doesn't need to. Her boss is expecting her in tomorrow, teaching a beginner's ballet class at 10am, and until then Li can avoid people all together. It's all she's wanted for a while, longer than she knows how to quantify.

She hadn't always been like this. But somewhere along the way it got easier to be alone and now as she spins across her bare floors, tossing herself violently around to a beat of an unfamiliar song, she thinks that she wasn't made to fit her edges against another person's. She's got too many corners, and none of them are soft – she's too sharp, too jagged, and she likes herself that way, angry and biting and dangerous. It's simple.

Aren't you lonely, Ben asks her in her head, and she thinks about it for the rest of the song, until it changes into something softer and happier, piano and acoustic guitar playing off against each other with two voices twining together. *Don't you miss me?*

She picks up her phone and pulls up his number. The last messages are from months ago, when they were still splitting their stuff up and organising going into their old flat when the other wouldn't be around, back when it still hurt to think of his name, let alone look at him. There's no unsent messages, haven't been for a while, and she doesn't want to send him one. For the first time in – too long – she doesn't think *how could you* or *why don't you love me* or *I miss you*, just *I'm sorry we couldn't fit together*.

Ana's sent a text, asking her to come over tonight – except that was four days ago, so Ana found her booty call somewhere else. Isabella texted to cancel their lunch this weekend, to which Li taps out a short **kk**, and when she scrolls through the rest she can't find a single one she cares about replying to. As she's looking, a new one pops up.

> **Ben: I miss you. We should talk soon, Li-Li.**
> **There's so much I have left to say.**

She reads it, thumb tracing over the letters of his name, of his words, waiting for her chest to seize and steal her breath, to make her desperately wish to hear his voice, to cave to his every wish just so she can hold him one more time, curled against him, his hands warm against hers. It doesn't come.

She smiles. Strokes her thumb across the screen one more time. Then she looks up and out of her window, December sun streaming down onto her, and she closes her eyes and sees yellow. It fills her, swirling across her dark eyelids, warm streaking into the furthest corners of her mind, to where the cobwebs lay delicately across old memories and unwanted thoughts. Her mind is golden and, when she breathes in, she tastes coffee on the tip of her tongue. The music goes on behind her, unchanged.

Li opens her eyes and taps the screen.

Message deleted.

1:23
Katie Wood

It's not like I *planned* on getting lost. It's just that Ikebukuro Station has so *many* exits, and so *many* people, and when you're tired and grumpy (not to mention short-sighted), Japanese characters merge into one big blob of colour. Or monochrome, as the case may be. I take two seconds to thank my lucky stars that I'm not in a bigger maze of a station like Shinjuku before searching for the right way to go.

"God damn it." I look around. I could try and find someone to ask but that goes straight against my aversion to looking like a tourist in this humongous city. The only thing I can use as a landmark is a vending machine which, in Japan, is not a rare occurrence. I swipe my commuter card and leave the bustling platform for the slightly more subdued station proper. People are still milling around, but I at least have enough room to breathe without feeling I'm going to pass out or shout at someone. Or both. Here, the stomping of feet and excited chatter is quieter and the pounding in my head lessens slightly.

Deciding that I'm probably dehydrated and that taking a break in my mad rush to get to where I'm meant to be will do me good, I slip into the slightly darkened area of the walkway and drop some coins into the machine, angrily jabbing at a heated almost-tea drink. I wait three seconds and when there's no indication of the machine obeying my orders, I jab the button again, harder this time.

"Come on, not today. Please," I beg the inanimate object. The lights on the display twinkle. "You son of a..." I push the machine, jostling the bottles inside.

I could give up the hundred yen and continue with my life... But that's not going to happen, not today. This would haunt me at night. Bracing myself, I give the machine one mighty shake and it teeters. My heart stops as it hangs in the air for a full second before crashing on its side, the lights flashing and then fading out of existence.

"Oops."

I take a deep breath and stare at the now flickering lights of the machine as it spills the broken bottles' contents onto the floor, the liquid seeping from the door hinges. The old rusted cable that's *supposed* to keep it from falling during an earthquake is no longer doing a thing. Huh. Someone should really fix that before someone gets hurt... or breaks something.

I look up to see if anyone saw me push the machine and catch the eyes of around thirty wide-eyed primary school children. They're all staring at me, their box-shaped backpacks weighing them down and their bright yellow hats like a landing strip showing the way for the authorities that are no doubt on their way.

"Uh... that... wasn't me," I say, and take off into the crowd. I have no idea where I'm going but I walk past about three bakeries and two entrances for lines that I know lead out of Tokyo before I get somewhere that is vaguely familiar. The green of the Yamanote line is a shining beacon of hope and I swipe my card and slip between the barrier doors, losing myself in the push of people and get on the first train I see, no longer caring which direction it's heading.

The jingle announcing the closing doors plays and we start to leave the station. I rest my head against the cold pole.

"My life is ridiculous."

At the next stop, I get off the train in an attempt to regain my bearings and, fearing that the police are now trying to track me down, I leave the station.

Across the street, in between the skyscrapers and flashing neon lights, is a quaint little shrine and a hunchbacked old lady waving incense through the air as she moves. The twin dogs that guard the entrance of the shrine bear down on me as I approach. I bow deeply once before stepping off the pavement and onto the cobbled path that leads to the ritual washing station, intended to purify you mind and body before entering the holy ground of the temple. Red banners flutter in the air as the incense starts to tickle my nose.

I stop by the incense pot, stopping just long enough for the scented air to flow over my head, and move towards the water, washing my hands and then mouth. It tastes sweet, not how you'd expect shrine water to taste, but I have to spit it out. I wash my hands again and, finally, I step up to the collection box, fishing a five yen coin out of my pocket and throwing it into the slots. I clap twice, bow once and pray. Two more claps and the ritual is complete.

I exit the shrine, enjoying the calm that settles over me and return to the station's entrance, turning to watch the old lady's practiced movements for a few more moments.

Through the noisiness of the crowd and the beeping of cars two blocks away, I hear the notes of her song lingering on the air. It has no words but the tune sticks in my head and feels like home.

In this bustling city filled with millions of people, surrounded by bullet trains and hologram information desks, sometimes you find little areas of history, and feel like you've fallen backwards in time.

I slip my phone out of my pocket and snap a picture of that little slice of history snuggled in between towers of modern living.

Now calmer and forgetting what I was so worried about in the first place, I return to the station, swiping my commuter card and staring up at the information board. When I'm this close, I can read it, but the letters still merge. I find the correct kanji combination for the station I want to go to and look across at the assigned platform. Platform 3. I take a quick look around to get my bearings and start moving, faster now that I don't have all those people from Ikebukuro station milling around me.

Movement breaks my moment of peace as a ruffled security guard runs up to me, shouting. I look at him in surprise.

"You're the person that broke the vending machine in Ikebukuro, right?"

"Uh… sorry, I don't understand Japanese."

THE LAUNDROMAT
Jonathan Fisher

I carried my broken laundry basket into the laundromat at 2:31 AM. The street behind me was dead; I hadn't seen or heard another car go past for the whole of my walk up the street. Up ahead, the road curved slightly to the left over the railroad tracks. The white, scuffed cross-guards were up.

I swiped a hand across my forehead to keep the sweat out of my eyes, and wiped my hand off on my jeans. I pushed through the door into the laundromat itself. The neon sign in the bay window next to the door blinded me.

Open 24hrs.

This time of night, there seemed to be more hours in a day.

I carried my basket of mixed clothes to the washer at the far end of the left-hand side aisle. There were two other people in the laundromat with me; a young woman who looked two heartbeats away from a meltdown, and a bearded, Middle Eastern man wearing a nice leather jacket. He had a cutting board balanced on his knees, and he slowly rolled cigarettes with old, arthritic fingers.

He met my eyes as I entered, and he gave a little smile. He saw me looking at his rolling operation, and gestured, "Interested? It's pure tobacco from Istanbul."

"Sorry," I said. "I barely got change for the machines."

"I get that." He smiled at me, and went back to his rolling. The woman ignored me. Part of me wished I'd ignored them both outright when I'd entered.

At this time of night, I know and see nothing. This is Florida; it's an easy way to catch a bullet.

But despite myself, I heard too much. I wished I hadn't forgotten to bring my headphones. When they didn't speak, the stuttering of the florescent light kept the place from feeling oppressively quiet.

"I don't know what else to say." Her voice was uneven with barely-restrained emotion. "I feel like I'm just repeating myself. Rambling."

"Ramble away," he said to her. He had the most paternal voice I'd ever heard. He sounded like the kind of person you'd go to hell and back twice to please.

I glanced briefly at her as I made the repetitive motion of picking something up from my basket and lobbing it into the washer.

She had dark skin, her hair was curly, her eyes were shadowed as the night sky beyond the windows and twice as mesmerizing, and her brows were drawn together in intense concentration.

I tried to ignore them both. They seemed to be having a moment. I didn't want to intrude. I wanted a lot, but not to listen. Besides, I had enough of my own worries to stew on. It feels like a tired old cliché to say its money and life, but that's what it I was.

I was living on my own for the first time, the stable job I'd had for three years went poof the second week after I'd moved out, and I was out of things to sell to keep myself in my apartment.

I needed something to break loose. But I had no idea what that would be. My dad, preacher through and through, recommended praying for wisdom.

Growing up in the shadow of him and that cross was enough to make that an impossibility.

So I sat across from the washer, and stewed on the problem. I'd figure something out. Maybe.

"I feel bad for even considering that," she said.

"In what way?" He asked.

"I'm afraid you'll be disappointed in me." Her voice was fractured and uneven.

"Hey, why would I be disappointed in your asking for help? I'd be a damn awful teacher if that's how it was," he said, gentle as a breath of wind.

"That's how it is," she cried, her voice shivering. "At least, it is in my experience."

He was quiet for a moment. "I'm sorry about that. From my perspective, it sounds like it's something you really oughta say."

She made a pained noise in her throat and I tried not to draw attention to myself as I threaded coins into the slot and pushed the tray in to activate the washer.

The machine rattled and banged and lurched as it came to life and I flinched. "Sorry," I said, and didn't look at them.

They didn't acknowledge me.

"I am afraid," she finally said.

"Fear isn't bad."

"All I was ever taught was to not be afraid. To not be angry."

"Tell the sun not to come up."

"No." She coughed and turned her chair a little, it squeaked on the floor.

"No, really, I actually want you to tell the sun not to come up."

"It can't be done."

"Then what makes you think you have any greater chance of not feeling things?"

She said nothing.

He continued, "Feelings are neutral. I mean they're not, but I think you know what I mean. They're just feelings. Now, you act under the influence of those feelings, we have a conversation about good and bad decisions. But having those feelings is never wrong."

She weighed that carefully. So did I, if I'm honest.

She seemed to relax a little, and then said, "That makes a lot of sense. I still don't know what to do."

"What are you trying to do?"

"Ease the pain in my heart."

"Ah." It was a loaded statement and for the life of me I don't know how he articulated so much in such a simple expression.

She plowed on though. "What's the point? I can't make my ends meet, no matter what I do. I hurt, and I can't make it stop," she said. She sniffed, "I have dreams and I'm trying to make progress but it seems like the choice is to either survive, or to dream. I can't do both. Not and live."

He considered. "How do you define progress?"

"Being able to support myself. Being happy."

"Good goals," he said. "I'm not even sure they're counterintuitive."

"How do you mean?"

"I think you can do both."

"How? I can't play this game and keep my conscience clean."

"There's absolutely nothing wrong with desiring stability and safety. Why do you feel guilty for that?" he asked.

"Because money is evil."

"Love of money is. But you described safety, happiness, stability. Why do you connect that to greed?"

"Because it takes money."

"For now, everything takes money. Craving stability doesn't make you greedy. And it isn't bad."

She slumped against the washer. "I'm so tired."

"Rest."

"Sleep doesn't fix the tired I feel," she said.

I let my shoulders sag. I had my back to them. Sleep doesn't cure the tired when you go to bed with nine dollars in your bank account and wake up overdrafted because of 'service charges'.

He made a noise of agreement in his throat.

"I don't know what to do. I feel so powerless," she said.

"Power is dynamic. It ebbs and flows."

"It seems to always ebb," she laughed, and it was pained.

"Kid," he said quietly. "You're tryin' to do too much."

"I don't know any other way. If I don't try to do it all, nothing gets done."

There was silence between them for a long moment. I shouldn't have been there, not really, but the conversation between them seemed so close to home for me that I couldn't move away. I couldn't not listen. I needed to hear more. Because the older man seemed to possess wisdom I hadn't heard before. Not like this.

If he had an answer, I needed it as much as she did.

"I know how much you hurt," he said at last.

"You are in a singular position to make it stop."

"That's never been how this works."

"Then what is this?" She looked up, I glanced at her, she looked at me, I looked away.

"This is the conversation you need to have."

She said nothing.

"Listen, it's noble to see injustice and want to fix it, right? I'd say that was something close to righteous. But it's not your job to save the world."

"No one else is."

"Well now you're just wrong," he said. "There's millions like you, trying to fix their corner of the world."

"It doesn't seem to be working."

"You're missing the point." He remained patient even though she was starting to get obstinate. "How would you save the world? Hmm? What unilateral actions would you implement to make that happen?"

She was silent for a long moment but when I stole a look at her, it wasn't because she was glaring him down, but because she was pondering.

She inhaled to speak, but he cut her off, "Wrong," he said.

"You didn't let me talk!"

"You're missing the point."

"You're looking at a problem you've already got a solution for and I don't have all the facts you're working from."

"That's fair," he said, cocking his head. "I apologize. I see it this way: it's not your place to save the wider world. Because that doesn't work. I mean, there's a few broad things you can do that helps. It's a start. But if you're gonna be the actual King of the World, then what's your tax plan? How do you manage the border skirmishes? How do you negotiate between warring neighbors who have equal claim to the same land?"

She had no answer to that.

"You see my point?"

"I think I might."

"The world isn't yours to save. Because you can't save a world. A world is a collection of parts. But those parts? You can mess with those parts until the end of days."

"I'm trying."

"Not yet, but I think you'll start to."

She sniffed.

"Why don't you intervene?" she asked quietly, hesitantly.

"Is that the question you haven't asked all night?"

"Yes."

"Why makes you think I don't?"

"Six million died."

"How would I have stopped that? Divine intervention? Smited 'em?"

She didn't answer. Her silence seemed pointed.

He took a slow breath. He'd whittled the pile of tobacco down to a few scraps that he rolled into an open cigarette, and he rolled it slowly. He was silent for a long moment as he put the cigarettes in a plastic bag, and then everything into the cloth bag at his feet.

"It goes back to that King question. Where do I draw the line? Folks have free will; where is the line between meddling and protecting?"

"You stop the genocide!" She threw her hands up. "If two dogs are fighting and you have the power to pull them apart, you do it!"

"I agree, but we're not talking about that, are we? Because if we've gotten to that point, how many other moments have I missed to intervene? And when is intervention meddling, as opposed to protecting?"

"You didn't answer the question though."

"No," he said, and he sighed. "It's not a theoretical. The genocides always happen."

"And you don't stop it."

He weighed his words for a long time before he said, "A crowd is an anxious beast, and it gravitates to the meanest and loudest voices because, when you're scared, anger and vengeance seem safe. Trying to pull a crowd that wants to riot apart is an easy way to get stomped to death."

She didn't respond.

He sighed, "I wish I could meddle with the crowd. But that's not how it works; it's never how it's worked. I don't do crowds."

"That's patently untrue."

"I'm going to gloss over the fact that you just called me a liar and instead point out that I inspired better orators. I find qualified people, and they lead people to a better path. But me personally? I'm not the spotlight guy."

"That feels like a copout."

"It kind of is. Free will is a helluva burden, kid, because it means in a lot of respects, I can wash my hands of your behavior."

She scoffed. He shrugged.

"But like I said. I find qualified people and give them notes. And they lead."

"It's not enough."

"It was enough in Selma. It was enough at the Stonewall bar. It was enough at Gettysburg. And any of a thousand other moments in history where somebody stood up and said, enough's enough."

"So that's your story, and you're sticking to it?"

"Why wouldn't I?" He smirked. "It's why I'm here."

She hesitated, "You really mean that."

"Yes," he faced her, I saw him do it and I focused very hard on watching my washer. "Kid, I'm not here for an object lesson. You asked a question, I'm trying to answer it."

She weighed that for a while.

"Here's the abridged version: you can't save the world because the world is a teaming mess of incoherence. But you can save individuals. You can help individuals."

"If I save the person, I save the world," she said quietly. "One person is a world."

"Precisely."

"How do I save myself?" she asked.

She asked for me, too, though she didn't know it, and in the heartbeat of silence before he answered, I was so acutely aware of my own pain it nearly drowned me in a silent surge of internal agony.

I clenched my teeth, put my hand to my mouth and squinted my eyes shut so hard I saw dots. And then the wave passed, and he spoke.

His voice was kind as he said, "Recognize you're playing the longest game in history. And if you're gonna put yourself in the position to be the orator, or even to *help*, you gotta survive today first. So you knuckle down, you do what you gotta to keep yourself alive. And then you do something that feeds your soul. You do the thing only you can do. And you do that every day and you watch for opportunities and you strike when you can. Repeat those steps until the spotlight's on you, not your forebears."

She sniffed. So did I.

"I'm sorry for doubting."

"I'm not. Doubt makes you ask the questions you otherwise wouldn't. And that means you get the answers you wouldn't otherwise get."

"Thank you," she said.

"Anytime." I heard him get up. I shouldn't have eavesdropped but what he had to say was important, and if I could maybe get a number, an email address, maybe he'd be willing to talk to me, too sometime and—

BLUE PENCILS

I turned around, but both were gone.

BLACKOUT
Jessica Kelsey

The square box-room flickers with neon green from the billboard outside. Sharp shadows dance between the loose flesh of the peeling walls. Above us, the ceiling sags with damp and in the corner is the brown, stinking evidence of another having used this room.

I sit with my knees tucked beneath my chin, watching the blue triangle glow on the inside of my wrist. Beside me, Logan lies still, his golden hair and fair skin glistening with grease in the dim neon light. We're lucky to have somewhere private to rest; we searched for hours to find this little room, on the top floor of a derelict high rise. There are others in the building - I can hear them shuffling and shouting and snoring below us. But this little room is empty. We don't mind the glass that litters the floor from the smashed window. Our skin is thick enough to withstand it.

I pick up a shard with the pad of my thumb, pressing the sharp edge into my hand, testing its strength like they used to do at school. It was a game, to see how much damage they could do to the Whirr before the teacher noticed. Not that the teacher cared. Once, Bram managed to get his nail beneath my eyelid. He tore my whole cheek down to my lip. I had to be in surgery for a week, and I still have the thread-thin white scars where my skin was reattached.

The lines almost glow against my dark skin, as bright as the blue triangle on the inside of my wrist. The clues I'm not quite human, the signs that earn me extra stares.

That's one thing I don't miss, sitting here in the half-light, wishing I didn't have the receptors to smell the rust and dust and the gas leak, not to mention the piss, the shit, and the smoke. There's no one here to chivvy their children away from us, or to stare at us like we're freaks in a circus show. Everyone here is too focused on their own survival. Their own problems are far more important than two Whirrs just trying to find their way through this city.

Here, there's a thousand more colours than the sterile pastels of the colony could even imagine, deeper and darker and putrid. Here is the sewage of the solar system, the factories churning grey-clad, dead-eyed workers into smothering smog; the rats skewered on spits, their fat sizzling; a fly sucking the juice from the eyeball of a baby-sized corpse. Here is where the dregs of humanity come to fester.

We dreamt of a new life beginning here, amongst all this poverty and decay. We were arrogant, thinking ourselves untouchable by death, who holds all the power here.

I shouldn't be in this city. I should be at home with my head plugged into a fully charged dock, dreaming a simulation of my father. I wonder if he will ever know what becomes of me. Maybe he expects me to be dead already. The last time I saw him is imprinted in my memory. I play it back to myself when I succumb to regret.

Opposite me, Dad hunches over his mug of coffee, idly swiping through his feed on the screen set into the kitchen table. His unbrushed hair collapses in a grey mop over his forehead, the left side pressing against his scalp in an indent from his pillow. His hooded eyes have the drowsy glaze of an early morning. He doesn't notice the rucksack by my feet, or the way I kept glancing at the numbers on the microwave clock. He can't see the nervous energy skittering through my wires as I count down the minutes before my rendezvous with Logan. He just sips his coffee and waits for a call from a client.

I want him to do something, or for him to say something; anything to make me change my mind and stay. But he just sips his coffee and answers the call, so I creep from our home, to where Logan is waiting.

I blink. The scene changes.

She smiles at me, that toothy grin with the dimples in her cheeks. She wobbles on her roller-skates, her red-streaked hair swishing back and forth. She holds my hands, our arms outstretched as she drags me along the white corridor.

Eva.

She told me to remember everything I feel towards my father is artificial, simulated by a processor. The deep ache in my chest when I remember his stupid jokes, and when he let me paint his nails and braid his hair. The clawing at my throat when I recall all the times he took me up to the observation deck and taught me the name of every star and planet and satellite in all the constellations. The terrible knowing that he will never again make me pancakes in the morning, just so I could smell their scent filling the kitchen, with the tart sweetness of blueberry jam. He made pancakes every morning, even though I couldn't eat them. He made pancakes every morning, even though he had to throw them away once they got cold.

"They pretend to love us like their own children." Eva's voice echoes in my head. "But they aren't fooled by us for a second. It's us who are the fools, for making the mistake of loving them."

I should have listened to her. If I had, then we would have all escaped together. She would still be alive. She would have known what to do about the batteries, while sitting in this little room surrounded by a thousand shards of glass.

I hated my father when he told me what happened to her. I wanted to scream, to break out of my cumbersome body that entrapped me in cold confines of plastic and metal. I wanted to curl up in bed and forget about the existence I was stuck in. I wanted to pretend that I didn't have to face the reality of our life, as nothing but a technological advancement to appease the childless middle-aged.

It would have only been a matter of time before Logan and I ended up like her. Discarded by the very people we trusted to love us unconditionally. We couldn't stay, knowing that once our childhood ended, so did our lives. We chose to live. We chose to run, but we ran straight from the frying pan into the fire.

We ran away, then we ran out of electricity.

Before he plugged into his dock, Logan told me that we'll leave the city tomorrow, to find somewhere with a clearer sky. "We need solar power," he explained, while setting up our docks on the floor, "Just enough to charge our batteries, and then we can build the generator." He smiled at me, his warm, beautiful smile that sent sparks shooting through my wires. "We're going to get through this, Astra. Don't worry."

I couldn't find the words to tell him I wouldn't be going with him.

We had a dream, Logan and I. A dream that was ours, not our parents', or a simulation. We had a dream we would build our own colony on this planet, out of sight of the satellites overhead and away from this city of industry and death. A colony for people like us. People with the same chemical emotions and thoughts as humans, but welded into mechanical bodies, as if that steals our right to be labelled as anything but objects. In our colony, we would all be equal. We would all be human.

It was a good dream. I couldn't bring myself to end it. I couldn't bear to see the brightness fade from his eyes.

I'd seen it once before. I'd been the one to tell him about Eva. It was excruciating, watching the meaning in my words sink in with every tic, every tremble, every spark dimming from his irises. His blue, beautiful irises.
I couldn't tell him about the batteries.

I'd been keeping them in my bag, while his was full-to-bursting with all the parts for the generator. The plan was to charge from our docks while we built it. The plan seems so naive now; concocted from the pristine confines of our bland bedrooms, as flat and stale as the rest of the stagnant satellites, where everything is mellow and soft and floury, and I didn't have to count every wasted watt.

In the spice and bite of this city, far below the satellites which block out the sky, where the rich live in lukewarm luxury, we've been burning through our batteries. We've used up all our energy to survive in this place, among all that's bitter and sour. Where scavengers scrape for survival among crumbling skyscrapers, insects picking each other apart for scraps.

I didn't tell him we only had one battery left. One battery, but two docks. He has a warm, beautiful smile, the kind that sends sparks shooting through my wires. I couldn't tell him.

Before this, I've only ever had to keep one secret to myself. I kept it for three years, eight months and fifteen days. I never told my father. I never even told Eva. I kept my secret deep inside, buried under fake smiles and white lies.

Logan is my best friend. He knows everything about me, except my two secrets. He doesn't know I've been in love with him for three years, eight months and fifteen days. He doesn't know I'll be dead when he wakes.

I sit with my knees tucked beneath my chin, watching the blue triangle glow on the inside of my wrist. Beside me, Logan lies still, his golden hair and fair skin glistening with grease in the dim neon light. The blue glow is dying. I can feel myself slowing down. My receptors numb. I close my hand around Logan's. The blue triangle flickers.

The light fades.

NO PLACE FOR ODIN
Anna Dempure

Frigg tells me that they do not speak of this on their return, that this was no place for Odin.

***

It is known that the moment her first child came into this world, the entire forest held its breath. With Frigg's grass still on her tongue, she wrapped her baby and made the long journey to the heart of this woodland. The Ash tree had been chosen to accept her gift to the gods and, as she dug, half delirious with exhaustion and joy, she thanked each and every single one of us.

It is known, that when this child died, she came to this very spot to weep. She dug again, and this time we wept with her. Maple leaves the colour of blood fell through her as she bargained with the same gods she had thanked half a year ago. We could do nothing but watch.

It is known that the second time she had brought a child into this forest to thank the gods, she could not bring herself to smile, and when she made the same journey another six months later, she could not bring herself to cry. She is with us now, a third time. *A final time*, we hear, a whisper not quite lost to us.

***

They straddle the two worlds, perched on the branches of her tree. Odin's birds have come a long way for this, summoned from The Other. Thought and Memory.

We can do nothing but watch.

She kneels, her knees supported by us, her hands in our embrace.

They watch her too, with unwavering devotion, black feathers shining silver and green.

She digs with tears in her eyes, her throat closed around the gust of wind inside her; the baby sleeps, wrapped against the storm inside her lungs.

Black bark smothered in moss. She is never alone in this forest made of her flesh; her blood runs through these trees. Odin's birds feed on the fallen fruit around her: their journey was a long one.

It begins to snow. Thick, sticky pieces of ice silently land and melt in her hair. Frigg takes her shawl and wraps it around her. Odin's wife has tears in her eyes. She looks to us, then to Thought and Memory, and holds a finger to her lips.

***

The woman doesn't look up, but at once becomes a paradox as she begs us, curses us.

She whispers a prayer to the hole she's digging. Thought and Memory return to their perch, elderberry blood smeared across their beaks.

She has called us here to be heard. When she speaks, the forest grows silent, and she wipes the mud from her hands and folds them onto her lap.

It's like she took the fabric of time and wove it into something new. Not something beautiful. But new, Frigg would say a century later, when she re-told her story.

***

The woman says, her voice now a well-known melody to the brand-new life sleeping on her heart, that she has given us, all of us, everything she ever had. She says that before she gifts the gods with another piece of her soul, we have to promise to stop. Just stop. She gives in to the unrelenting need to sob that has plagued her since the moon went dark. She is enchanting, the woman on her knees. The enigma in our gut.

Frigg hides the tears falling from her eyes. She shakes her head, and kneels by the woman; she takes her in her arms and buries her face in her hair. Frigg cries with her.

This wasn't our doing, she whispers. It turns into a gentle breeze, lost to the woman.

***

She tilts her head back; she cries beneath Odin's birds and the dangling obsidian. The crystal tree glimmers above her, each branch catching the light of the silver clouds. She looks from one to another, from moonstone to amethyst. They tell the story of her loss.

We can do nothing and neither can they. The song of Odin's birds is high and broken: they cry for her, they cry with her, they cry so loud they can be heard in The Other.

Shhhh. Frigg holds up a hand to silence their wailing.

"Can you hear me?" the woman asks, voice cracked from disuse.

We can.

She is no longer compelled to dig. She picks up what is left of her first and second offerings. A fleeting look we do not catch.

She takes the wooden box by her knees and empties it into the hole.

She begs us without speaking. The worst kind. The loudest.

We hear you. We can do nothing. Some things we cannot control.

She blows out the candles. She breaks the circle and leaves; the hole remains half dug. She doesn't look back.

Frigg tells me that they don't speak of this on their return. She says that when she got home that night, Thought and Memory went straight to bed. She says that this, really, was no place for Odin.

THE BEEHIVE
Alec Tudor

Deep down, there is a stage. It's like a globe of gold, huge and unending. It is marked by black lines, and great minds burn in every section within its walls.

There are multiple balconies, up, down, and upside down. There are seats left, right, vertical and horizontal. There should be a door that leads to the exit, but everybody has forgotten it. Nevertheless, everybody's gathered, from thieves and inquisitors to madmen and scholars. Some of them sit down, some of them higher, some of them highest. They all see the same thing.

The World's Theatre is ready to begin.

"What a charade!" screams Chekhov, as he sits down with his gun in place. He's annoyed by the exaggerated details of this theatre. Vakhtangov disagrees; he claims the how, not the what, is what matters. Suler has fallen asleep from too much mediation. Kubrick is stuck with his typewriter and doesn't complain; Tarantino reads the Bible. Kazan, as usual, bangs on the wall, yelling for a play he doesn't need to revise. "Will one of you salesmen give me the new Streetcar?"

"At least you are not arguing with novelists," says Kubrick.

A few knocks from above: Nabokov and King are curious about the adaptations.

Meanwhile, to the left, Beckett gets painted by Dali through the wall; both speak French but do not understand each other. Ionesco says no to everything. Tennessee Williams is stressed by Kazan and is trying to impress him; Odets swaps jokes with Clurman. Sartre and Camus, as usual, are having a boxing match, while Ibsen is laughing at their futility.

Upwards, the novelists are arguing over typewriters. Woolf gives an expert's perspective on the issue, but gets bored midsentence and instantly switches to the simpler perspective of a 3-year old. King is annoyed by Kubrick and lets his typewriter rest after a 63-hour marathon. Salinger doesn't give a damn. Tolstoy is confused again. Kurt Vonnegut starts describing his typewriter, but goes on about how he drove through the galaxy with this cool girl who was tripping on something and was working in a clothing store down 45th Avenue.

Frank Zappa randomly hears it from his box to the right. Of course, the song cannot be heard, as Hendrix is tripping again and rocking out random notes, whilst Bob Dylan is stuck in the wall between poetry and music. Thom Yorke is listening to Aphex Twin and is feeling cultured and interesting.

Suddenly, a beggar wanders through the audience.

"Oi! Stanislavsky! Come back here!" screams Chekhov, getting out of his chair.

The beggar doesn't answer.

"Stanislavsky? Ah! Be damned!" screams Vakhtangov, who gathers with Chekhov.

Of course, Stanislavsky is no more; only the beggar remains.

All sorts of exhibits wonder and call for Stanislavsky; the entire actor's quarter screams for him – some in appreciation, some in rage.

"Stanislavsky? I'm no Stanislavsky, I'm a beggar!"

The director's quarter protests; Stanislavsky is first and foremost a director, and actors shall not imitate him!

The playwrights intervene, claiming The Method is the antithesis of the play; they cannot conceive the actors and directors knowing the characters more than them.

The philosophers start debating the meaning of this.

"But where are you heading now, gentlemen? Why all this argument?"

"I am not going to sit in this cage while that Stanislavsky wanders around!"

"Who's responsible for this?"

"We need to find out the truth! Who has it?"

"It must be the actors! They're the dumb ones!"

"But how can they hold the truth?"

"We need to get out of here!"

"I don't like that Cioran fellow!"

"Me neither!"

"He might know how to get out of here!"

"Could he?"

"Just get them all!"

They jump at each other: Plato curses the politicians and strikes Voltaire, who is still trying to establish an absolute ruler in this play. Aristotle curses the poets and still hates democracy, so he strikes Plato. Nietzsche disagrees with everything and proceeds to attack everyone. Of course, Camus and Sartre have punched themselves through the wall, still only content with each other's company.

From the playwright's corner, Ionesco is the first to lead the attack. Ibsen contradicts him by detailing what is real and possible and what is not, but is struck by Thomas Reid of the Scottish School of Common Sense. Alan Bennett retaliates with a swift punch to the head. Down goes Voltaire, while Odets falls to a kitchen knife. Nietzsche's voices have paralyzed him, as he hits himself as much as he hits the enemy.

The ongoing battle is joined by loud bangs at the wall. It's Kazan, who runs into Sophocles. Kubrick is not interested and is still typing, while Tarantino and Vakhtangov team up on Kierkegaard. He falls, as God isn't responsible for his existence.

The actors outflank all enemies; they start chanting about their greatness, until the directors, playwrights and philosophers decide to band together and kill everybody, expect their model wives. Ayn Rand objects, but is beaten up by Marlon Brando. Ray Liotta gets into a brawl with Al Pacino. De Niro tries to wrestle Tarkovsky, but his hidden gun is empty, so Tarkovsky gets the upper hand.

Roars and screams fill the battlefield, as all try to escape; all end the same way, and the audience laughs.

Bangs are heard from the back wall. New enemies, presumably. The wall cracks with a boom. They are bloodied, and fewer in number.

"Well, who the hell are you?" says Aristotle.

"Who the hell do you think we are? Scientists."

"Have you found the truth?"

"No evidence of it, no."

There is silence. Both groups stare at each other in bafflement.

"Your science claims to know the truth!"

"Our science seeks to find it. Your art only seeks to lie."

"Liars indeed, they are. Maybe we should dissect their bodies and see if they hold it or not."

"They must hold it. Otherwise, there is no way."

"But what if it's you who are hiding it?"

"They must hold it!"

"What if there's none?"

Silence.

"Then kill them all!"

The artists attack.

"We might not have the numbers, but we can certainly even them out!" says Hawking.

The scientists attack.

"A prize for the one who deals the killing blow on the last of these liars!"

And so, Nobel throws his dynamite, and they explode.

43

The rest march on the fight reaching momentum. Unfortunately, Marie Curie finally crashes from her negligence and drops her potions. The air turns toxic with gas, and they struggle to run. They start coughing and dying. They bump into each other, trying to find the enemy and escape; none do. None do.

Nietzsche tries to reach the audience, but alas, he crashes into the wall!

Kubrick is still writing _ still on the stage. He doesn't care for all this drama. In the back, Shelley Duval approaches him with an axe.

"Time for some real pain..."

All are dead. All now wonder. The wall is not yet broken. The World hesitates.

"What else is there to see?"

"Nothing; they have all killed themselves. The bastards, they have all killed themselves!"

"Why were they doing that?"

"Why? Why? Why!"

The audience erupts in protest. Where is the show? Where is the spectacle? Where is everything?

"Let's get out of this place!"

"But how did we get in?"

The air is filled with silence.

"There must be... an exit."

"Where is it?"

"Someone must know!"

"Who's hiding the truth?"

"Out with it, the liar!"

"Could it be him?"

"No, it's not me!"

"Get it out, you liar!"

"Beat him until he says it out loud!"

And the poor odd-looking boy gets killed.

And they all fight among the balconies; down, up, and upside down. Blood flows through the seats left, right, vertical and horizontal. The wall breaks.

"You!"

Run, you! Flee this place, for it will fall down! Search for the exit, should there be one! And if not, die trying! But don't come back! No, don't! The show is over; the world's theatre is over —

CHECKING INTO HOTEL LONELINESS
Eimear Lawlor

My grandpa told me the hardest thing about getting old was that he didn't have a roadmap for old age. When I was younger I had a roadmap for my life, but somewhere the route changed.

Now I sit on a hard bed with a soft purple headboard. Together they didn't seem to fit.

A red neon light on the opposite building flashes: *Girls, Girls, Girls.* Three red and blue girls dance kicking their legs high in a can-can. For a few minutes, I am mesmerised, wondering about these iridescent girls. Are they real? Of course, they're not, but there are girls just like them somewhere. Probably in that building, waiting for lonely, drink-dependent men to call. Or maybe it would be some juvenile who wanted to see what it was like to be with a woman. He might have been fantasizing about some Russian girl, while his parents watched telly downstairs.

I pull my knees in close to my chest and take slow shallow breathes. The musty smell of damp and stale cigarettes makes me nauseous. A spider weaves its way across the faded, embossed wallpaper _ the type bought in the 80's because it'd looked posh. Above the window, a bluish-black mold reminds me of a liver, or maybe the scythe of the grim reaper. I stare at it for a few minutes _ the grim reaper looks ready to knock on someone's door.

I shiver, my feet now cold, the excuse for a duvet offers little warmth. I rock back and forth. I pull my knees in tighter, and the duvet falls away. I look down at the chipped red varnish on my toenails. I don't care.

When I went to the hospital to have my children I always painted my toenails, even though my feet were the last things the obstetrician would be looking at.

The neon sign flicks on and off, perhaps a loose connection, so it flashes *–irl, Girl, –irl.* Its message is still clear though. The potential clientele won't care; they aren't looking for perfection. In their alcohol or drug-hazed utopia they want to escape reality, and if that includes a pretty woman, that's just a bonus.

The pipes gurgle as hot water tries to push its way through the aged air-locked plumbing network. A bead of sweat slowly drips down my forehead, but I doubt the room has heated up _ the tip of my nose is cold, my fingers are cold. The thin-walled room shakes as a door somewhere on the same floor slams shut, followed by a woman shrieking.

"You bastard! You haven't paid me. I've got to feed my kids!"

Laughter and footsteps past my door. "Whore."

My chest tightens. My breathing quickens, and the room starts to close in on me. Would the kids be waiting for her at home? I think. No. I push their memory away like an unwanted itch, an itch that hurts and bleeds when scratched.

The light spills from the streetlight onto the bed, it narrows, and the walls begin to slide towards me. With the rise of panic, I look at the bedside locker. Its watermarked surface doesn't have the habitual bedside lamp hotels always provide. I doubt there's a Bible either.

I cast my eyes around the room. Where did I put it? The dim light, coupled with my inability to focus, makes it hard to see if I had put anything on top of the chest of drawers. Finally, I see the Xanax at the bottom of the bed. I grab the bottle, my hands trembling, and unscrew the lid. Half a Xanax would do, just to calm me for the moment. It always helps. I move my tongue around my mouth to stimulate my salivary glands. It takes a while, but eventually, it does the trick and I drop the other half on the bedside locker.

It takes effect. I feel like I'm with the men in the building opposite, lying back against the soft headboard I wait. It was easy to imagine what went on in this room. What drove people here? Was life that lonely? Or did they need to fulfil some depraved fantasy

The manager had not been able to hide his surprise when I asked for a room. He gave me the hourly and nightly rate, I told him I wanted it all night. He had pushed his fingers through his tobacco-coloured greasy hair; his raised arm revealed yellow patches of dried sweat. When he spoke, he shoved his chewed rollie out with his tongue.

"Ye've to be out by ten am sharp." Throwing me the key he went back to reading the paper. "Cleaner 'av to go in before ten," he mumbled, his interest in me gone.

Soon my breathing slows into a regular rhythm. Calm now, I stretch my legs out and flex my feet, the stretch in my calves feels good. Angry voices filter up from the street below, a mixture of accents, all speaking in English. No, it isn't an argument, just a delivery. Doors slam, and a truck engine roars to life, fading into the night.

46

The Xanax bottle lays open its bottle, its contents spilling out onto the duvet. I pick it up, and with my other hand I drop the tablets back in one by one into the bottle. I count them. My breath now stable, my forehead dry.

***

Over the past year, I had seen three different doctors in various parts of Dublin. I gave small personal inconsistencies when I filled out the doctor's registration form. Nobody checked. I looked presentable. Middle-class accent with kind of up-to-date clothes; Zara isn't expensive. I faked utility bills. It's easy to modify any document with the help of a half decent computer.

"Yes, doctor. It happens every day, it's so hard... I find it hard to breathe... I dunno doctor, I just feel tired and like crying all the time."

He gave me the prescription without batting an eyelid. And so did the other two. One of them could hardly spell Xanax and had to Google it.

***

One-hundred. I drop the last tablet into the bottle and throw my legs over the side of the bed and stretch before I go to the sink in the corner.

The street is quiet now. The sign on the opposite building still flashes. Something moves and stops in the middle of the room. A mouse. I don't move. It doesn't move. We start a staring game, both of us eyeing the other, wondering who's going to move first. The mouse looks away, scurrying into its safe place somewhere dark and secure.

The glass beside the stained tap looks clean, I flinch at the cockroach lying on its back, its six legs upright and rigid.

I fill my glass and avoid looking in the mirror. I know my eyes will question me.

Back at the bed, I'm cold and pull my cardigan closer. I take the other half of Xanax from the bedside table and throw it into my mouth with a small bit of water. I hold it in my mouth for a few seconds

I look at my watch 8pm, we'd arranged to meet at 9pm.

***

I'd heard about Blendr from excited mums outside the school gates.

"No strings attached," they giggled. "It's quick and easy!"

The Xanax starts to work, I feel good. My head clear, clear of horrific thoughts, blood, screams, sirens they float away. It's good. One more. One, two, maybe three.

A drink of water. This is nice. I listen to the night, things I'd never noticed before when I was here. The noises infiltrate my head. Lorries stop and start. Bin lorries. Deliveries.

There's a knock at the door. I don't feel like getting up. I'm in a good place. I hear my name, another knock, the door handle rattles. He says my name again. But that's not my real name.

AN UNUSUAL UNDERTAKING
Roger Jefferies

If it was a painting, one of those pale-washed Scandinavian rooms in the nineteenth century, Stephen would be seen from the back. You would have to imagine his face as he looks out through the wide window. Beyond the glass a large garden is depicted, with an oval lawn, framed by large trees in the last stages of autumn. He seems to be staring at it.

At the end of the lawn is a neat pile of bronze and gold leaves. The room is a kitchen, and Stephen is leaning on the draining board of a sink, his hands spread out along the edges, thumbs on top. From the light, it's probably morning.

***

Every morning, just before he goes out, he stands there like that.

"Don't, don't," she'd shouted when she ran outside. But she's not exactly in the painting, if it were a painting. He sees her though, as she was, just then.

He had opened the door and run after her. She stumbled by the bottom bed and fell in the swept-up leaves. That's how he sees her, in the pile, which was disturbed by the fall. She was face down, well, partly, and the leaves settled back round her face and nose. She didn't move. He had caught up just at that moment, breathing heavily, still angry.

"Get up, you fool!" he said.

That's why there are still leaves down there, in the same pile. He can't bear to sweep them up, and they stay there to remind him of when Rachel left for good, left him, and life, at the same time.

Her mother had died in her fifties; she'd had a weak heart, and a sudden embolism took her off. When you fall in love, he thinks, you don't consider those things. You believe life stretches out forever, and Rachel wasn't like her mother or anyone else: she was fit, a swimmer, and she played tennis all year round. He thinks it's incredible she fell over and died at her age, but that's how he explains her death when he tells people who ask; it was probably inherited, her condition.

He lied at the inquest, or, rather, didn't tell the whole truth. He said he'd looked out of an upstairs window and seen her lying in the leaves.

Since that day he's been numb, not entirely conscious. He's not opened the post, which lies in a stack on the sideboard. He's not played squash or watched football. He's upset the neighbours.

He moves slowly. The cleaner will be in later. She'll empty the dishwasher and do the ironing. She's taken pity on him. But would she have done if she knew? She was attached to Rachel, not him. He hadn't spoken to her much in those days, just a greeting on the way out to the station in the mornings if he met her coming in. But now he takes a later train and doesn't get up at seven any more.

Going to work as he used to do, he knew the people standing on the platform, but the nine-thirty is an unknown train. The best thing is that he doesn't have to see Toby, who always catches the earlier train. Toby came to the burial and stood on the other side of the grave, not looking at him. Stephen wondered if he was thinking how near a miss he'd had, or even that he might be feeling sorrow. At least Toby's wife cried a little; there was a hanky in her hands as the wicker coffin, with Amy's wreath on top, was lowered slowly into the grave. Afterwards she came in for a drink, but Toby went off.

He thinks about his daughter, Amy, who is coming to see him at the weekend; she rings up every day to see how he is. It's kind but it's unnecessary. There's nothing to say. Except she asks him about the will and what he's done about it. He persuaded Rachel that they ought to make wills only a year ago; whether it was just luck or a premonition, he doesn't know, and it's the same with the life policy he'd organised through the firm two years ago. It's in trust to keep it outside death duties, and the underwriters accepted her as a normal risk. He's going to inherit it all. It's conscience money, he thinks. Her conscience.

He had a bad moment when the gardener told the cleaner about finding the knife, in among the hostas. It was left for him on the kitchen table, with a scrappy note. He picked it up and looked and remembered holding it, and then throwing it away when he knelt to turn Rachel over onto her back, to feel for her pulse. When he saw it again he didn't want to touch it, but gingerly held it between his finger and thumb and quickly put it in the rubbish bin.

That day of the death it had been on the draining board and he was shouting and shaking, all was clattering in his head, her words, her sudden ferocity, her dislike. He must have picked the knife up, he did pick it up, he grabbed it, he wanted something to emphasise what he was feeling, and he lifted it and stabbed, and stabbed in the air. She shrieked and ran outside. No one knows that. To everyone he's the unhappy widower, and the family, what's left of them, are still together as they used to be.

He'd roared at her. He can roar from the touch-line and sometimes in the office. He drives hard bargains. Amy just tells him to button it. But his son Martin is like his mother. He went back to Cambridge as soon as he could get away.

In the evenings when he returns from work, the house is silent; it smells polished. He goes to the kitchen and stands at the sink and looks out. The pile of leaves looks sullen in the evening light.

When she comes on Saturday, Amy chides him for not opening his post while she puts some flowers she's brought into a vase and fills it with water under the kitchen tap.

"Here," she says, picking up the post and bringing it to the table. "Do it now, while I'm here."

He looks for a knife to slit the envelopes. He remembers the other knife, and his rage. He's weary now, and doesn't want to be bothered with any chores. He simply can't understand why it all happened. He's spiritless. He exists, but he feels he's not quite alive.

When some of the envelopes are opened he finds that the effort of reading the contents is hard. The words don't seem to mean much. In the office it's the same. Although it's another world where he is someone else, the regional director, he can't keep up with things. They want him to take a rest, but if he didn't have the office to go to, he doesn't know what he'd do.

"Shall I do it?" Amy says.

He pushes the letters over to her. He gets up and makes some tea.

She sorts the condolence letters into one pile. Others are addressed to her mother, and she puts those into a second pile. There are other letters and bills, bank statements, and she makes a third pile and starts to open them quickly. One she doesn't. It's marked 'personal' and she mentions it when he sits down with a tea tray.

"It looks a bit formal. Shall I open it?"

He nods and hears the rasp of the knife against the paper.

"Oh dear." She sees who it's from and what it's about. "You'd better read it."

He takes it from her and tries to focus on the words and then grasp the sentences.

"I don't understand this."

"Give it to me. I'll read it properly."

He looks at her, waiting. She nods her head as she goes down the paragraphs. He drinks his tea.

"What is it?"

She puts it down and puts out her hand to find his across the table.

"Dad, did Mum talk to you before she died?"

"Of course she did."

"Yes, but I mean, did she say anything?"

"I can't remember," he says. He does remember.

"What happened, Dad? I know she fell over and was dead when you got to her. But before that? Try and remember what you were doing, what she was doing."

He doesn't reply. He sees Amy and Martin clutching each other by the graveside and then hearing the vicar say 'dust to dust', and all he wanted to do was jump in the grave and stamp on her.

Amy speaks to him very gently, "Tell me, Dad."

He starts to cry. He can't stop himself. He's ashamed and shakes his head. Amy gets up and looks for a box of tissues. She finds one next to the toaster.

Amy holds his hand again. After a while, she says, "Mum spoke to me a few months ago. I told her that she must tell you herself. It was going to be terrible for Martin and me. And for you."

Still weepy, he considers what she has just said. She knew; they've both known, her and Martin. Only he didn't know, until Rachel spoke to him, smoking furiously, two cigarettes at least, before she ran out of the kitchen throwing one wildly, half-smoked, onto the floor. He does remember; it's almost all he thinks about.

He wipes his face. "Toby was her bridge partner. She said I ought to know she'd had an affair with him. His wife had no idea. Your mother was going to leave me that day, walk out, just like that. She wasn't going to him, she said, but it had made her realise that, now you'd both left, she didn't want to live with me any more. I had no idea she felt like that. I didn't believe it. There was no warning."

"Did you roar?"

"She gave me a document from some lawyers. She said it meant that her half of the house was hers. Then I shouted at her. She said she'd taken money from the joint accounts, she'd found a flat to rent. I shouted more."

Then he starts to lie again as he did at the inquest, "I went out of the room and went upstairs. Her suitcases were packed. I looked out of the window, like I said, and I saw her on the ground."

But it wasn't like that. He saw the knife and lifted it and stabbed it in the air and roared and went towards her and she fled, and he chased her down the garden and she fell. But no one knows.

Amy looks at him and starts to cry herself. "She'd been to the doctor. There was fibrillation; it was explained at the inquest."

"I didn't know anything about that. She never said."

Amy blew her nose. "You didn't say that she was leaving you at the inquest."

"It wasn't fair. She rushed at it, and she didn't warn me, just tried to leave, that day. People were sorry for me and I was ashamed to say she was leaving me, in front of them. No one knows now. Why did she want to go? What did I do wrong?"

She sighs. "You stopped noticing her, Dad. She was unhappy; but she didn't love that man, honestly. It was desperation, she said. Martin and I haven't known what we could do. She didn't want us to do anything. She said you and she would still love us and she'd talk to you about us. But she didn't, did she? All she did was to make a new will, leaving half the house to us two. It's in this letter from the solicitors."

He feels crushed. Rachel did all this behind his back. Angry again, he thinks she should be dead.

Amy pulls out one of the other letters she's opened. "The insurance company say they won't pay out on some policy because they didn't know Mum had seen the doctor and had a heart condition."

His business is insurance. He knows what the insurance company means. There wasn't proper disclosure to the insurers about Rachel's health. He sees now, how she prepared everything. She took what she wanted. But then, he thinks, she's dead, and she never got away after all. I've kept her. In the eyes of the world I'm better as a widower than as a deserted husband.

They stay at the table, saying nothing. He pours her some tea. Across the garden, when he looks up, he sees the fallen leaves on the actual spot, shining in the weak sunlight, with their autumn colours.

She says, "It's hard when everything we take for granted comes to an end. I can't get over it, that she should be so looking forward to something in her life, and then she drops down dead. I'm sorry I didn't tell you, Dad. But I really did think Mum should talk to you. When she made up her mind, she was like a lamb, leaping about doing things. She didn't think about you, only about leaving you. Didn't you see that?"

He didn't see it. He was used to her; it was comfortable. Not being married to her is unthinkable, not imagined, ever. But now he isn't married to her, their separation is permanent, in the grave, not in the divorce courts. His pain is double; but, all right then, he says to himself, perhaps she's better dead than alive. Better for me.

"Don't worry about the house. Martin and I don't want to sell our share; stay on as long as you like," Amy says.

It's humiliating to be in the place on their sufferance. But he thinks it wouldn't sell easily now. He'll have the last laugh on them.

"Shall we go down the garden?" he says. "I walk out nearly every evening."

He gets up unsteadily. She takes the flowers out of the vase. The air is wintry and still. The sun is scarcely warm. She takes his arm, and they go across the lawn slowly.

Close up, he sees his commissioned metal structure with sculpted copper and bronze leaves fixed onto a round frame, fastened into the ground.

"It's so pretty this, Dad, it's sweet. It looks like real leaves from the house. I'm sorry the neighbours made a fuss. I like it anyway." She puts the flowers down gently beside the sculpture. "Mum loved the garden; she said it's the one thing she would miss."

"Now she needn't," he says. "I didn't want her to go. Now she'll always be with me."

"I know."

"It was better than anything else. Burying her here, where she fell. In my own garden, in spite of the neighbours."

"It's lovely, Dad."

"I like it too." And at night, he thought to himself, I can walk here, open my fly and piss on her.

KICKSTARTER

As part of the funding for Blue Pencils Vol. II, we launched a Kickstarter campaign. We had an overwhelming response, and it took less than a week to reach our funding goal. We are incredibly grateful to everyone who donated: without you, this book would not exist. But particular gratitude goes to those special backers who paid the highest amount.

We offered different tiers of reward, the highest of which offered backers the chance to send us their short story prompts and have us write them their own story. Here follows our attempts.

STILL WATERS
Charlie Wilson
For Gill Parys

At night, the water rushing over the top of the lock keeps her up. She lays in her bunk, staring at the panels above her, wishing that the gentle rocking would send her to sleep; instead, it just makes her stomach churn (although, to be honest, that might be more about the absence of the small huffs of breath that she'd come to expect). She still tries, every night without fail, to lie down and wait for sleep to claim her. It never does.

At around 2am, Morwen rolls out of bed, leaving twisted sheets strewn behind her, as if she'd been wrestling with more than just her insomnia. She climbs out the front doors of the boat and plops down into the deck chair, pulling a woollen blanket around her shoulders. Curling her legs under her, she reaches down and pulls baccy out of the compartment. She holds the filter between her lips as she taps the baccy out, spilling some over the edge of the rizla. It drops to the floor beneath her feet, joining crumbled brown leaves and a few shreds of torn paper. The moonlight is enough to see by, but from here she can't make out any words. It's a good thing, really.

Once she's rolled the cigarette, she puts it between her lips and lights it. The first pull always makes her cough, even now, months after she started. It's part of why she only smokes at night, when no one is around to see her. The other part... Well, she doesn't like to examine her behaviour too closely.

At 2am, the towpath is empty. Not that it's ever very busy here – she chose this mooring for its abandoned, overgrown bushes; for the potholes and mud and gravel under foot; for the absolute lack of care that spoke to her overdramatic side. But still, during the day, there are a few travellers. Sometimes they're the hardened wayfarers, who hold their windlasses with callused palms and have farmer's tans. Other times, they're anxious looking hire boaters, mumbling under their breath as they try and operate the lock with poor to no instructions. They're rare; no self-respecting company would send them up here (not all companies are self-respecting, though). The rest are lost, waifs and strays with no home to call their own, so they find a section of hers to enjoy themselves in. The highs vary, but the looks in their eyes never do.

It's not what she planned. But these things rarely are.

Smoke hovers around her head. In the haze, all she can see is the orange glow of the cigarette, hanging limply in her hand. It's 2am, and she can't sleep.

***

In the morning, she gets up just after 7am. She doesn't remember the last time she slept for longer than three hours. The skin around her eyes is tight, itchy, and her eyes are so dry she fears that, if she blinks, she won't be able to open them again and her eyelids will be glued shut. It's fanciful, but she's inclined to be fanciful these days; there's no one around to laugh at her and pull her out of it.

She goes through the motions: there's no water for a shower, so wet wipes make do, then she ties back her braids with a band and avoids looking too long in the mirror. Her clothes are running ragged at the edges, fraying at the too-long hems, but they don't smell any worse than the rest of her boat. When she finishes, she heads to the stove to boil the kettle, but when she flicks the lighter it doesn't ignite. She's out of gas, out of water, out of energy.

It'll mean a trip to the shops that she doesn't dare think about, but she's almost out of tobacco and there are only three cans left in her cupboard, when she checks. One of said cans is pea and ham soup, already three months out of date, and the other two are baked beans. She digs a bit further and turns up a Fray Bentos pie, to add to her small pile. It's not enough to last a week, she thinks. Okay.

The best way to do something you don't want to do, she's found, is to not think about it. So she doesn't think about the shops as she shoves her feet into shoes and picks up her bag. She doesn't think about the people she'll have to interact with as she checks her purse. She's low on cash – perpetually, to be fair – but this necessitates a further stop at a cash point along the way, which will add several minutes onto her potential for interaction. She's not a fan, but it has to be done, so she makes sure she has her credit card and clambers out of the boat, locking the hatch behind her.

To get to the main road, she has to climb over the lock to the towpath side, then it's a brisk six-minute trot to get down to the nearest bridge. She climbs up the rickety stairs – noting the new tags that have appeared on the wall since she was last here – and turns left, pulling her hood up. The local

Tesco will do well enough. It starts to rain as she walks, just the light, fine mist that barely counts as rain but is still enough to make her miserable.

It's another three minutes on the main road, then she turns left again, and crosses the road at the zebra crossing. A taxi has to stop as she walks, and he lets his car roll forwards until it's almost at her feet. She considers stopping and making him wait more, but doesn't have the energy for it. Safe on the other side of the pavement, she takes the next right and finds herself in the car park.

She keeps her head down as she goes to the cashpoint. She's in luck – there's no queue, so she goes straight for it and puts her card in. Pin number fine, she considers checking her balance, but there's really no point. She chooses cash instead, and gets out £40 – enough for her shopping today, and she really doesn't want to carry much around with her.

Her next challenge, once card and cash are safely stowed, is running the charity gauntlet. There's a woman sat behind a table, cheerfully knitting away in a bright yellow mac, as if she's not fussed by the rain steadily soaking her wool. It's important not to make eye contact, so Morwen ducks her head as she marches for the door as quickly as possible. The woman isn't faint-hearted, however, and calls out to her.

"Excuse me? Hi," she says. Morwen makes a rookie mistake of glancing up at the noise and she's caught. The other woman is freezing, her cheeks and nose red and lips visibly chapped, but she still somehow looks cheerful. "Hi," she says again. "You look miserable!"

Morwen doesn't really know what to say to that, so shrugs. The woman doesn't take that as the discouragement it was meant as, though.

"I'm Elaine, but you can call me Elsie," she is told fervently. "Can I ask – have you ever knitted or crocheted before?"

Unwittingly, Morwen thinks of baby blankets and a crocheted octopus. Something must show in her face, because Elaine – Elsie – smiles and says, "It can be comforting, right? Were you any good?"

Morwen shrugs again, then feels obliged to actually contribute to the conversation. She mumbles, "I was alright."

If her smile before had been too cheerful, it's now blinding – the ferocity of her grin makes Morwen consider abandoning her quest and returning to the cold Frey Bentos pie. Only the idea of rickets has her stand her ground and wait until the wattage decreases.

"That's excellent!" she exclaims. "We need more knitters, especially ones your age – so long as you don't mind hanging around with us old biddies!"

Given that Morwen would put Elsie as around 45, she finds that a bit odd, but doesn't interrupt. There's no need to make this longer than it has to be.

"We meet twice a week at the old mill, down by Gapley Lock – do you know the canal?" At Morwen's nod, Elsie continues. "Tuesday and Thursday, 6.30pm start, tea and coffee provided and we have a weekly biscuit and cake schedule. We'll tell you all about the project when you arrive-"

And that's her cue to interrupt. "I'm sorry, but I'm not interested." She says it as firmly as she can, but she can't quite meet Elsie's eyes. Rejection has never been her forte – not that she's had much experience in it, truth be told.

"Oh," comes the reply. Morwen can't bear to look up. "I understand. No worries at all – listen to me prattling on!"

Morwen shifts her weight uneasily. "It was nice to meet you," she mumbles and takes a step towards the door.

"Wait," she's told, and then something is shoved towards her. It's a flyer, and on top of it is a ginger nut wrapped in a napkin. She blinks up at Elsie in confusion.

"Well," the woman says with a pragmatic tilt to her voice, "You look half starved, love. Eat your ginger nut and take the flyer – if you reconsider, we can always use another pair of hands!"

Morwen takes the biscuit – and the flyer – and manages to dredge up a facsimile of a smile for the stranger, whose grin wattage is back up to full beam despite her disappointment. Morwen nods uncomfortably at her and heads inside to pick up her shopping.

***

When she gets back to her boat – *Still Waters* – she fits the new gas bottle first. Tea is her priority here, but she loads up her electricity as well and flicks the light on, just because she can. She unloads the shopping while she's waiting for the kettle to boil – mostly cans, again, but she bought potatoes and bananas and fresh bread, too, as well as butter and milk. Her left hand has painful red lines on it, from holding the shopping bags, and her right aches from lugging the gas back, half full because she couldn't lift the full one. She needs to get a delivery, but who delivers to boats? They're not exactly permanent addresses.

The kettle whistles and she pours water into the biggest mug she has. It's twice the size of a normal mug, and all black with tiny kittens on it, utterly obnoxious and stupid – and she loves it. She heaps in two spoons of sugar and a small dash of milk – just enough to colour it, but not enough to actually weaken it, and stirs furiously. The teabag goes on the pile of old, dried out ones, and she makes a mental note to deal with the bins. It's starting to smell in here, and if she gets more mould she'll never be rid of it.

Tea in hand, she sits down and pulls the napkin out of her pocket. Ginger nuts are perfectly dunkable, and she thoroughly enjoys the biscuit, but she doesn't like the twinge of guilt in her gut. She finds herself worrying the edge of the flyer, and pulls it out of her pocket with a sigh. It reads:

Do you like to knit? Are you wool crazy? Can't get enough of crochet? We want you!
We're looking for knitting and crocheting enthusiasts to help with a project of MASSIVE PROPORTIONS. Must love teamwork, tea, and happiness.
Join us Tuesday and Thursdays from 6.30pm at Gapley Mill for fun, friends and lots of wool!

Massive proportions… she sighs. There's no point fretting over it, but she can't seem to help herself; Elsie had been so very enthusiastic, and the idea that Morwen hurt her feelings makes her miserable. It's not that Morwen has a problem being rude if the situation calls for it, but to upset a polite stranger is a bit – well.

She shakes her head and puts the flyer back in her pocket. She might as well take her mind off it somehow – and she's been out of water long enough to be well aware that she smells. She'll move *Still Waters* and get a refill and pump out.

***

It's not until three days later, when she's putting a load of laundry on, that she finds the flyer again. She'd thought about Elsie a few times, but she's good at not thinking about things she doesn't want to, these days. So when she pulls it out of her pocket, slightly dishevelled and crumpled at the corners, it's actually a surprise. She wrinkles her nose – her jeans are definitely stinky now, and could probably stand up on their own.

With a heavy sigh, she sinks down onto her bed. It rocks the boat slightly, and she makes a mental note to get to the Chandlery and buy a new main line as soon as possible. Hers is fraying at the edges, and it's not exactly a great idea to be without one. She rubs her thumb over the flyer and sighs again. It would be a terrible idea to go. She'd feel awkward and embarrassed. She's not slept properly in weeks – she's not suitable to be in public. She hasn't picked up a crochet hook in a year.

And yet the clock is ticking towards 6pm and she can't help but look from her jacket to her shoes. She ate a late lunch, so she doesn't need to eat. And Gapley Lock's only a 20-minute walk. Morwen looks from the abandoned pile of laundry to the clock and for the first time in almost 11 months she gets up and moves.

The clothes are thrown in the washer and soap tossed in after. She changes from her pyjama trousers into leggings and a loose tunic, throws her mac and wellies on over the top – it's been raining for a week straight, and she's not risking trying to clamber through the mud without wellies – and then hesitates over what to take with her. She doesn't have any supplies on *Still Waters* – she brought nothing with her – and no time to get some. Actually, she doesn't even know where she would go around these parts. She's barely explored farther than the canal and Tesco.

Rather than focus too closely on that point, she shoves her purse in her pocket and the flyer in the other. Her keys, cork balls an all, go after and she leaves her boat rocking as she strides off.

Within minutes, she's absolutely soaked. But she doesn't let it discourage her: she pushes on, head down and hood up, until the chimneys of Gapley Mill are in sight and she feels a little flicker in her stomach, anxiety soaking in with the rain. It would be so easy to turn around and go back to bed, which might not hold sleep but is warm and dry.

She doesn't. Morwen crosses the bridge and heads for the door, which is propped open by a brick and letting the rain in. She stops just outside, peering inside anxiously, but the rain pushes her to gather her courage and step inside, where the sounds of laughter usher her down the corridor and round a corner.

There's a room with a hand-written sign on it that says 'WOOLSTERS ONLY – ALL WELCOME'. Morwen's lips twitch at the contradiction, and she pushes it open.

The five women inside stop talking and turn to stare at her. She recognises Elsie at once: she's in a bright yellow dress, cheeks bright red and hair loose around her shoulders, a sort of frizzy halo. The other four are strangers. The eldest, a woman who must be at least eighty, is tiny, black and serene looking: she has a bright pink scarf wrapped around her head, at odds with her sober-looking black dress. The woman beside her is only slightly younger, white with blue-tinted hair and the largest glasses Morwen has ever seen.

The other two are younger, both with hair that's still only half grey. One is white, probably mid-fifties and overweight, with bright red lipstick and half a ball of wool wrapped around her hands as she tries to de-tangle it. The other is Indian, wearing a turquoise sari, probably around 60. All of them are staring at her, mouths slightly agape.

"Hi," Morwen says, giving a little wave. "I have a flyer?"

It's a ridiculous thing to say, but Elsie jumps to her feet with a wide smile. "Hello! You came!" She hurries across the room, turning her head over her shoulder to speak with her friends. "This is the girl I told you about!"

Morwen isn't sure how she feels about being talked about, but she tries to keep a smile on her face as Elsie reaches her and grasps her hands warmly, tugging her into the warm gently but firmly. "Hi," she repeats redundantly.

"Let me introduce you!" She tugs again and Morwen stumbles forwards, towards the circle of chairs. "This is Parvati," she says, gesturing to the Indian woman. "And Mary, Lillian and Norma." She gestures in turn to red lipstick, large glasses and pink headscarf. "Ladies, this is-"

"Morwen," she interjects, before Elsie falters too much. "It's nice to meet you."

There's a resounding chorus of similar greetings, and Morwen is ushered into a seat that's hastily dragged from one side of the room to join the circle. It's rickety, one leg slightly shorter than the others so it rocks underneath her as she sits down, but it holds under her weight.

Once they're all seated, Morwen waits for someone to speak. The expectation in the air, however, quickly dims as they all cast glances around, waiting for someone else to breach the void. Morwen curses herself, briefly, for the idea of leaving her warm, dry, blissfully empty boat.

"So," she offers quietly. "I heard something about a project?"

Elsie's eyes light up as she leans forwards on her chair, and says, "What do you know about yarn-bombing?"

***

When the article in the paper comes out, Morwen can't help but smile. She stops at Morrisons on the way back from work – she took an event manager position at a charity three months ago – and picks up six copies, then reconsiders and adds another couple for her friends at the marina. It's a brisk 20 minute walk, but the sun is shining and the breeze is warm and gentle, blowing her hair out of her face. She puts sunglasses on and tucks the papers under her arm, one headphone in her ear blasting the Arctic Monkeys. Twenty minutes melt away and she's home before the sun even starts to dip towards the horizon.

She waves to Ron and Tracy, who are sunbathing on top of their boats, and gets lazy waves back. Morwen drops a paper onto their stern deck, tucked under a bucket to keep it safe from the breeze, then heads to *Still Waters*, which is shining in the sun. She finished painting it just this week, and gone are the rust patches and general air of misery: the outside is a sleek silvery-green, and the name is now nestled into a bunch of carefully painted sunflowers. She just needs to finish re-painting the gunwales black and then her boat will look as merry as can be. The rainbow-coloured knitted cover for her tiller helps.

Inside her boat, she rushes to get ready before she has to leave. She rinses some tomatoes she picked this morning, from the plants that she tends to atop her boat, and hastily prepares a salad that she wolfs down. Then she changes out of her work clothes, throws on a loose dress, and roughly finger-combs her hair to clear the knots out. She smells of lemon and it leaves a smile on her face as she clambers back off *Still Waters* and leaves the marina.

The door is open when she gets to Gapley Mill, but she doesn't hesitate to enter this time, merrily calling out her presence for any who would hear. She gets back a cheerful chorus of welcome – there are fifteen voices calling to her these days, not five. The core troops are still here, though: Elsie is in a knitted yellow jumper that Morwen helped her create the pattern for. Mary and Lillian sit, surrounded by a tangle of wool, happily complaining as they wrap it back into balls. Norma leans over the shoulder of one of the younger girls, carefully watching her to see where she's going wrong. And Parvati is laughing, her daughter at her side, who grimaces as she pulls the thread from a crocheted mass to undo it.

"Look what I found," Morwen tells them, dropping the pile of papers onto an empty chair. She pulls one open and reads aloud: "Notorious Activists At It Again."

"Hah!" Elsie shouts from the other side of the room. "'Notorious' my left tit!"

There's a response of general mirth and Morwen grins, reading on. "Infamous activists, the Woolsters, showed up in Birmingham this week, protesting the recent change to disability laws. The Woolsters are renowned for their 'yarn-bombing', a form of protest that involves covering objects or structures in public places with decorative knitted or crocheted material.

"Leader of the Woolsters, Elaine McMillan, had this to say: 'Our protests will not go unheard! To rob disabled people of their rights to free parking is tantamount to taking away their rights of movement.'"

"Here, here," Norma shouts from the corner.

"The Woolsters," Morwen reads on, ignoring her hecklers, "Recently protested the US President's visit, and are known more widely for their street art outside both the Houses of Parliament, and the houses of previous and current Brexit ministers."

Elsie calls them a word that it's better not to repeat. There's another round of laughter, and Mary glares ferociously at Elsie, but Morwen barrels past it. "So, we're famous again," she says.

"Infamous," Norma says cheerfully. At 89, she's the oldest member of their group. "I want that on my headstone, you know. 'Here lies Norma, infamous Woolster'."

Someone else chimes in with a retort, but Morwen focuses instead on the article. The picture is possibly her favourite part – it's the core six, standing in front of the town hall, each strewn liberally in rainbow wool. They took part in their protest, this time, and Morwen smiled at their focused faces, all passionately chanting their slogans.

She brushes her fingers over the picture, then reads the caption. *From left to right: Elaine McMillan, Norma Johnson, Mary Williams, Lillian*

O'Reilly, Parvati Singh and Morwen Jones.

THE OBSERVER
Anna Dempure
For Lyle Skains

When she put her hands around the basket of figs and reached inside, I felt my stomach drop.

"…and you know that this is how it ends?" she asked, pulling out a light brown snake.

"Yes. I'm sorry," I said. "If you survive, he'll parade you around the empire as his prisoner."

She turned away from me.

"I'm sorry," I said again.

"Don't be."

And when the Cobra wrapped around her wrist, its fangs aimed towards her golden throat, I held my breath.

"Don't look!" I said to her children and tried to pull them closer to me; their faces pressed against the raised patterns of the stone. Her youngest traced the patterns with one hand and sucked the thumb of his other. His eyes were soft and wet. Dazed. His nose ran past his suckling lips.

She gasped when the snake bit into her neck, and then she looked at me. Her youngest was still tracing the history etched into the walls, but the twins turned to me and buried their faces into my dress. They were older. They understood.

I cried when I watched Cleopatra kill herself. I took her children; I hurried them out of her chamber and into a room cast in golden stone, with a stream of fresh water running through it. It flowed directly into the sea.

I stopped just at the edge, by a patio divided by white lace curtains – so opaque they looked like smoke. I knelt down and kissed all three of their wet faces.

"What will happen to us?" Selene asked. She had her mother's voice.

"I don't know," I lied.

"Will you stay with us?" her brother asked, his voice barely above a whisper. The rays of the setting sun caught in his irises; they looked like set amber.

"I can't stay, Helios. I can't."

***

If you go to Alexandria: on the crumbled stone ruins that made up a tower, overlooking the Mediterranean, you'll see the exact colourful patterns Cleopatra's youngest son traced with his fingers on the day she took her life. If you keep walking into the stone ruins, you'll find a slab of untouched stone with my face etched in hieroglyphs.

***

It's not the only place you'll find my face. It's in a leatherback book, in one of the back rooms of the Registry office in Nantes. You'll find it faded onto a page of paper made from recycled Senegalese cloth. You'll find it in a section designated for Aline Sitoe Diatta, along the shelf labelled as 'Possible Conspirators'.

The morning of May 22nd, 1944, I left Aline's cell in tears. I left her after she had taken her last breath, after I had wiped her face with a lukewarm cloth, and swatted away the flies, after I had yelled for the guards.

In the moments before, when she drifted on the verge of consciousness, I kissed her fluttering eyelids and wiped the tears out of my eyes.

Then, I swore an oath: "They will try to erase you from history, to burn your face from the recesses of their minds. I won't let them. I will hold onto you. I won't let you be forgotten."

The morning of May 22nd, 1944, I walked through the streets of Mali, of Timbuktu, breathless. When I had first met Aline, she was in Kabrousse, Casamance. She had been standing in a rice field, ankle deep in mud, her arms spread out to the heavens, drenched in a torrential rain storm.

"You see! She's the rainmaker!" a man had shouted from the crowd gathered around her. "Our rainmaker!"

"Why do you do it?" I asked her almost a year later, as we walked under the canopy of some ancient Kapok trees. She had a limp, and so we meandered down a dusty path at a leisurely pace. She changed direction and walked towards one of the trees.

"Do you know what we call these?" she asked me, running her hands along the thick, eight-foot tall roots.

"Fromager," I replied, walking towards her.

"That's what the French call them. We call them étufay. Some Diolas call them busanay, others bosanobo. Each name is heavy with meaning, weighted in this land, in our history." She leaned her weight against the towering roots. "You asked me why I do what I do, and that's your answer." She tilted her head back and closed her eyes to the dancing leaves, to the darkening clouds. Since Aline had brought back the rain there had been a downpour every day. We were expecting another one.

"I don't understand," I told her.

"It's our tree, it has always been our tree, and yet no one can remember its names. The only names it ever knew until they arrived."

I didn't know what to say.

"If we can't hold onto the names of our trees, how are we meant to hold onto anything else? Do we even exist where you're from?" She ran her left hand protectively across the tree's bark.

"Yes," I told her.

"Is that it?" she asked me, her eyes still closed against the clouds.

"You exist, but there is so much that was lost. So much that never made it to my time." My voice grew heavy. I wanted to cry. "Your descendants will know your name, they will name buildings and ships after you."

"But?"

"But, almost all of them will never be sure about how to speak this language, or how to bury their dead, how to bless their babies or the many names for your medicines and herbs and dishes."

"And I can't change that?" She stepped away from the tree, took one final look towards the sky, and we resumed our slow pace back towards the village.

"Aline, you're not the first woman who wants to know how to change her fate, but you are the first whose fate I would do anything in my power to change. But I don't know how." I looked down at the bronze coloured dust that was all over the Casamance region and tried not to show her that my eyes had filled with tears.

"I already know my fate. It's not my fate I'm trying to change. It's theirs." She nodded towards the people rushing around the village, trying to get home before the coming rainstorm. "...And their children's, and their children's children."

***

"I know I'm going to die here." That's what she told me the first week in the prison cell in Timbuktu. "You could have told me this is how it ended," she said.

"I can't do that. If I ever told any of you how it ended, then you wouldn't live your lives."

She laughed like I'd never seen her laugh before – her head pushed back, her face rounded in a smile.

"You should know me well enough by now to know that nothing would have stopped me doing what I did. The French couldn't stop me, and your predictions wouldn't have either."

"I know that now." My smile was cracked around the edges.

***

It was August 21st, 1614, when Elizabeth Bathory told me that her hands were cold. I told her it was nothing to worry about, that she should get some rest.

I helped her take off her corset and laid out what was left of her petticoat on the cold stone floor of her cell.

"Talk to me, please." Her voice was heavy with tears.

"What would you like me to say?" I asked her.

"What are they saying about me now?" She shifted on the straw mattress. She turned to face me.

I took the small three-legged stool by the door and sat by her bed. I took her hand in mine – her veins protruding, blue and twisted, like the ends of a frayed rope. She closed her eyes.

"Do you really want me to tell you the truth?"

She opened one eye, dark brown, although recently they'd developed a grey ring around the outside. But she still maintained that she had perfect vision.

"The truth. Tell me the truth. I have to know," she said, closing her eyes again.

"They're still accusing you of murder. They're still saying that you tortured and killed those girls, and they're still using Susannah's testimony."

She took in a deep breath. Inside her chest was a small wheezing sound. I pulled the rough woollen blanket further up and tucked it in around her neck.

"…And, what are they going to say about me where you're from?" She turned her head towards the damp stone ceiling. Tears beaded at the corners of her eyes, tracing little wet lines down her cheeks and onto the straw mattress.

I opened my mouth to speak.

"The truth, please," she interrupted.

I closed my mouth around the lies I wanted to tell her. I had spent the last four years with her. Since her arrest, all the way through her trial. I had grown to love her, as a friend, as a companion.

"Where I'm from some refer to you as the 'Countess of Blood'. They call you a vampire, a murderess, a cannibal. The stories of what you did have gotten more elaborate. There are more details in my time then there were at your trial. They say that you burned girls with hot tongs and then dipped them in freezing water, they say that you covered some in honey and threw ants on them, they say that you drained them of their blood and bathed in it to stay young and youthful. They say you ate them alive, bit their faces and arms and thighs."

She didn't speak for a long time. She wiped the steady stream of tears that seeped out of her closed eyes.

"Do you believe them?" she asked.

"No!" I went to sit on the bed with her. Her hand still wrapped in mine. "No, of course not."

"Why not?" she asked, pulling the blanket tighter around herself.

"Because, I know you. I know you'd never do anything like that. I know you didn't do it."

"When do I die?"

I took in a deep breath. I looked down at her hand in mine and ran my fingers across her ropey veins.

"Tonight," I said, and looked up at those steady brown eyes with the grey rings.

"Good," she replied. "Good."

***

Half a century after her death, an anonymous artist painted the trial of Elizabeth Bathory. He painted me in a red dress, but I was wearing green; he painted me with blue eyes, but mine are brown. You'll find my face at the corner, not facing the judge or the jury, but the servants testifying against a woman who would never be found innocent of the charges against her, not that day and not four hundred and seven years from then.

***

I held Lady Jane Grey in my arms before they executed her and wept in the crowd as they burned Joan of Arc alive. I was with Boudicca when she drank the poison that killed her, and I am at the back of every painting, every sketch and every grainy photograph in your history books. You've seen my face before; take a closer look.

THE COUPLE FROM ACROSS THE ROAD
Anna Dempure and Charlie Wilson
For Marion and Ken Balmforth

Her mother had just left for work, slamming the door behind her in a cloud of smoke and cursing – she was running late, again. Claudia had been left in charge of her younger sister, who was sprawled out across the shaggy orange rug in the living room, kicking her legs in the air as she scowled at the cartoons on the TV. When Claudia put a plate down in front of her, Minnie didn't even look up at her, instead craning her neck to keep her eyes trained on the screen.

Claudia went back to her perch by the window, using a sofa cushion as a makeshift table. She liked to sit on the windowsill, especially when it was warmed by the radiator beneath and she could curl her toes against it as she munched on her morning jam on toast.

Today there was no school, being a Saturday, but that just meant she could stay there longer, forehead leaning against the window, her sister watching cartoons in the background.

***

She first saw them through the white netted curtain of that window. They stepped out of a taxi, preceded by clouds of their breath in the dry November air. He scooped her up in his arms and nestled his face against her smiling cheeks; she wrapped her arms around his neck, clutching a small bouquet of yellow flowers in one hand. Then he spun her around, her long brown coat flaring out around her, and a white dress peeked out from underneath, with ruffles around her ankles.

"Minnie! Come see this – we have new neighbours!"

70

Her sister clambered to her feet, a piece of toast in her hands, and she licked the jam from her fingers.

"Do you think they'll have children our age?"

She dropped the piece of toast, jam side down onto the thick brown carpet, some on the cream peeling wallpaper by the radiator, and stuffed the remains of her toast into her mouth.

"Oops!" she said, spraying crumbs out of the gaps through her front teeth.

"Don't touch anything!" Claudia shouted, already running to the kitchen for a wet cloth. The last she saw of the couple was the man fumbling for his keys, still holding the woman in his arms. She was laughing hysterically, her head thrown back, a grin splitting her cheeks. When he found his keys, he nudged the front door open with his foot, and the woman shut it behind them with her free hand.

***

The next time Claudia saw the couple, it was a Tuesday morning before school, a few weeks after they moved in. She told her mum about the new couple from across the street, but her mum hadn't seemed impressed. She'd muttered about 'the nerve of them', and slammed the saucepan down onto the stove hard enough to make it *bang*. Claudia didn't ask her what she meant. But today, as her mother rushed out the front door, lighting a cigarette, she saw the couple standing outside their house. The woman was wrapping a scarf around the man's neck, and he kissed her cheek before walking down the road towards the bus stop at the corner.

"Morning!" the woman called, waving to Claudia's mum. Her mum puffed on her cigarette and ignored her. The woman's hand hung in the air a moment longer, a frozen greeting. Then, slowly, she let it drop and went back inside.

Claudia thought that, if she'd been outside at that moment, she would have said hello back.

***

By the following Wednesday, Claudia realized that the woman and her had the same morning routine. Whilst Claudia was almost always starting her second piece of toast, the woman was wrapping the man's scarf around his neck (to which he always responded to with a kiss on her cheek). Her mother had taken to standing behind Claudia with a cigarette burning, her leg in a never-ending twitch as she too watched the couple from the windowsill.

She never spoke to Claudia, but sometimes she'd say: "The cheek of it!" or "No respect..." And it was only once the woman had closed her front door that she would put her coat on and leave for work.

***

A few days later, when Claudia and her mother peeked through the netted curtain, they saw that the house opposite was covered in scrawling bright red letters. It was all over the front door and living room window.

"Isn't natural... I said it. Didn't I say it?"

"What happened?" Claudia asked between mouthfuls of buttery toast.

"Go get yourself ready for school, love." Her mum wasn't in a hurry to go to work today. Instead, she took Claudia's seat and lit another cigarette.

***

The next morning, her mum's friend was over. Tilly was a loud woman, with dirty blonde hair down to her waist. Claudia came down the stairs to find them at her windowsill, an ashtray where she usually sat already filled to the brim with cigarette butts.

"Who do you think did it?" Tilly asked, puffing out a cloud of smoke. It crashed into the net curtain, dissipating against the cool windowpane.

"Doesn't matter. They can do what they choose behind closed doors, but they shouldn't be flaunting it all over the street. It isn't right."

By the time her mother and Tilly had left for work, the house stank of cigarettes, and the white netted curtain had taken a slight yellow tinge. Claudia moved the ashtray to the floor and reclaimed her seat.

Across the road, the man was talking to two police officers, holding a brick in his left hand. He was angry, pointing to the red writing that his wife was trying to scrub off. She had a sponge and a steaming bucket of water, but the letters weren't shifting. The man pointed again, this time to the gaping hole in the living room window. By the time the officers left, Claudia realized that she was running late for school.

***

After a few weeks, the window was fixed and only the faintest outline of the words was left. Claudia could only see it because she knew what to look for. It was the New Year, and Claudia's mother had sworn that 1981 was going to be her year, but she'd lost her job in the first week of January and today she was say on the sofa with Minnie, watching cartoons and eating cereal out of the packet.

72

Claudia stayed out of her way, because these days her mother had a tendency to be extra irritable and lashed out at anything. It didn't take much to set her off. She'd said just yesterday that she'd enjoyed the New Year's celebrations too much and was still on a come down from Molly. Claudia hadn't ever met a friend of her mother's called Molly, so she wasn't entirely sure what she meant.

She hadn't seen the couple leave the house either, although she knew they were still there because sometimes she saw them moving around the house through the windows – all lit up in a golden light. One time she'd caught a glimpse of them dancing through one of the upstairs windows. The light had caught on the woman as she twirled out and Claudia had stopped, watching as they swayed together.

***

Two weeks later, and her mother had found herself another job. It was in a pub, which meant that she almost always stank of beer and stale smoke. She didn't get up with Claudia in the mornings anymore because she worked evenings, and so Claudia had her perch back to herself for her toast before school.

That morning, instead of kissing the woman on the cheek after she wrapped his scarf around his neck, the man brushed his hand over her stomach. Then, he kissed her on the lips.

Claudia walked to school thinking about that kiss.

***

It was a wet March morning when the whole street was woken up by shouting outside. Claudia, Minnie and their mother stood on the doorstep in their socks, agog as they watched the police running into the house across the road. When they pulled the man out, they pushed him to his knees. His nose was bleeding and it dripped into the grass. His dressing gown had come undone. The cold turned his chest red and pink. He spat out blood and tried to get back up, but a police officer pushed him down.

When they dragged the woman out, he tried to get up again. It took three officers to keep him down.

"Don't hurt her! Don't hurt her!"

An elderly woman watched the scene from the bus stop at the corner, peering out from underneath a clear plastic hat.

Everyone was awake that morning, some with cigarettes trailing from their lips, burning steadily, forgotten, and some clutched mugs of tea as they lent on their door frames in their pyjamas, watching the police raid the house.

"She's pregnant! Don't hurt her." They pushed the woman further into the cold. Claudia had never seen her with her hair out. A long black afro surrounded her tear-stained face.

Tilly ran over from three doors down, her slippers slapping the pavement. She had a steaming mug of tea in one hand, and a cigarette held between her lips.

"What do you think's happened?" she asked when she reached Claudia's house.

Claudia's mother took the cigarette from Tilly's lips and took a puff.

"Probably connected to the muggings that have been going on. She must know someone. Or drug smuggling, or whatever it is people like her do."

"Oh, do you really think so?" Tilly took back her cigarette.

Claudia's mum just shrugged. "Are you coming in? It's bloody freezing!"

ABOUT HUNDRED YEARS PUBLISHING

Hundred Years Publishing is a two-person team trying to bring diverse voices to the forefront of modern publishing. This anthology is our first publication and features authors from around the world. We publish a quarterly e-magazine, *Claim*, and our manuscripts include poetry, fiction and non-fiction.

If you are interested in our projects, want to take part or feel like getting in touch, you can find us at: hundredyearspublishing.co.uk.